PRIYA BAJPAI

AF579715

All rights reserved. This book or any portion thereof may not be reproduced or used in any manner whatsoever without the express written permission of the publisher except for the use of brief quotations in a book review.

Disclaimer: All stories compiled in this book are works of fiction. Names, characters, businesses, places, events and incidents are either the products of the author's imagination or used in a fictitious manner. Any resemblance to actual person/s, living or dead, or actual events is purely coincidental.

First Edition 2020

ISBN: 9788194847427

Published by ArtoonsInn Room9 Publications, India
Cover design by www.thearchaichouse.com
Typeset by www.thearchaichouse.com
Printed in India by Manipal Technologies Limited, Manipal

ArtoonsInn Room9 Publications

www.artoonsinn.com

To the victims of COVID-19:

Those who braved it and those who died fighting.

Foreword

When Priya asked me to write a foreword for her first solo book, I admit I was surprised. More than that, I was honoured and humbled by the trust she reposed in me to introduce the labour of her love to the world.

I've known Priya more through her writing and have always been amazed by the ease with which she waltzes through various genres and stylistic choices. She is one of those writers who can spin believable worlds through their words and her first solo book, Goya is a testament to that.

Goya is an Urdu word to convey the suspension of disbelief especially through stories. Having read Priya's stories, I have now experienced what exactly it means. Right from the first story we slide into a world that's so different from the one we live in.

As someone who's first book was an anthology of short stories, I know that losing a reader's interest is our biggest concern. My book, Hiraeth- Partition Stories From 1947, had the common thread of partition running through them with ordinary people caught in a mesh of extraordinary circumstances.

Priya's book, on the other hand, is a multihued anthology of twenty-seven delightful stories that reminded me of the bioscope wallahs of our childhood.

They would go from street to street with their makeshift contraption that had multiple viewing ports. Cupping the ports with their hands, kids would clamour around it to peek into the magical world as the bioscope wallah would yank the handle and spin a delightful tale.

The book promises a roller coaster ride through the unbelievably believable world of Geishas, time travel and Pharaohs. Allow yourself to be regaled with murder mysteries with unusual twists or explore the possibility of a young, new sun or step into Neil's shoes for a hair-raising paranormal experience.

I wish this book all the success it deserves and take this opportunity to present to the world a master story teller who's waiting in the wings to unleash her magic on her readers.

With much love and a lot of pride,
Dr. Shivani Salil
Author, Hiraeth- Partition Stories From 1947

Acknowledgments

I take this opportunity to appreciate the people who have played an instrumental role in helping me write this book. I want to express my gratitude to the many people who saw me through this book, to all those who provided support, read, offered feedback, assisted in the editing, proofreading, and designing processes.

My parents have always supported and encouraged my fascination with writing. They have always believed in me, and Goya would not have been possible without their blessings. I salute them for their selfless love, care, and sacrifice.

My heartfelt regard goes to my father in law and mother in law for their love and moral support. The one regret I will always have is that Pappa couldn't hold Goya in his hands. I know he would have been proud.

My siblings, Pooja and Abhishek, have always guided me. I appreciate their persistence and their encouragement. I thank them both sincerely, and I know that they will always be there for me.

Thank you, Aesha and Anshu for constantly motivating and inspiring me. Goya wouldn't see the light of day without you.

My heartfelt gratitude is extended to my friends, Moomal, Shefali and Shweta. I couldn't have seen this through without their undying love and unwavering faith.

I also appreciate the constant support of my friends in the writing circle. Thank you, Tina, Damyanti, Natasha, Jaya, Sreeparna, Sai, Anupriya, Aoishi, Ell P, Meha, Shivani, Sonali, Srivalli, Arva, Varadharajan, Sonal, Shweta, Fatema and Piya.

Thank you, Kanika for being my editor. Your keen insight has made Goya wholesome. Thank you for helping me to look at my work objectively. An extended thanks to Ashwini for her valuable inputs.

Special thanks to Shivani for graciously agreeing to write the foreword. It's gratifying to receive endorsement from a writer I admire and respect.

I am also indebted to the watchers of Room9. Thank you, Mithru, Husna and Khyati. It's because of your efforts and encouragement that I hold my dream in my hands.

My son, Anjaneya, has always been excited and supportive since the onset. On some occasions, he has supplied me with valuable insights. I see the spark of creativity in him, and I know he will achieve great things in life. Thank you for always loving me unconditionally.

Finally, and most importantly, I thank my husband, Vishal. He has always been an ardent supporter in all my endeavors. He is always the first to read my stories and his feedback has always been priceless. Thank you for making my stories and my life beautiful.

Introduction

Goya is an invitation to immerse yourself so deeply in the stories that they affect all your five sense and become real to you. So fasten your seatbelt and prepare for the rise through the peaks, valleys, and cliffs to a fascinating emotional landscape.

Contents

Kaleidoscope

The first thing Tess noticed about the room was its pungent smell. It always made her feel nauseous. The only thing she liked in the room was the sunbleached curtains, with remnants of bright colored flowers, which had turned pastel. The curtains, with their faded flowers and butterflies, dramatically transformed the room.

Tess spotted a patchy couch next to the window. *The couch and its location are just perfect*, she thought. The only problem was that it was occupied. A lady, not a day older than Lady Gaga, was sitting on it fidgeting with her mobile. *What a waste!* Tess decided to go and sit next to her. The lady wouldn't mind, Tess assumed. She sat next to the lady and murmured a hello, which the lady completely ignored. *Let's call her Aunt Grumpy*, she giggled at the thought.

Her mother took a seat opposite Tess and picked up a magazine from the desk nearby. Tess looked out of the window. *There they are!* A smile curved her lips again. That was when she felt the lick. A puppy appeared right next to her. It took her by surprise. She wasn't expecting them inside the clinic. *They didn't like the smell, they never came in before.*

“Sit still, Tess!” Mom shrieked.

She looked at her mother, wondering what she had done.

“I am just sitting,” she protested.

“No, you are not,” Mom said.

Tess nodded to keep Mom calm. When Mother went back to her magazine, Tess rejoined the puppy. Her eyes popped out when she saw it changing shapes. She had never witnessed a shape-shifter before. It grew a longer tail and a bigger face, like a hound. The big hound was almost ready to pounce on her. It bared its sharp, white teeth. She wanted to run, when she heard her mother whisper harshly through gritted teeth, “Tess, still! Now!”

Tess looked up, she didn’t see the hound. She looked out of the window again. The fluorescent unicorns were prancing in the garden and flying in the open sky. On her last birthday, when she met them for the first time, they told her that their magic was concealed in their horns. She wished to have a birthday party with them soon. *Ah! Only if I could speed time up,* she mused.

Just then, a dragon appeared where the hound had been standing a few moments ago. She was quick to name it 'fire fury'. *Giving a name should help to tame him, and then I should be able to stop him from being a fire-spitting monster*, she reasoned. It worked. When she saw the dragon wagging its tail, she knew he would not hurt her. She jumped up to stroke him.

"Tess! Can you stay quiet for a moment?" her mother snarled.

Tess wished her mother could see the world the way she saw it. Every creature was unique and beautiful. They all loved sharing their wonderful stories with her. She remembered how the neon nightingale sang the most mellifluous song on her birthday. That was her best birthday. All the creatures she loved, lined up to meet her, and to dance and frolic with her. They loved her, as much as she loved them.

Tess kept shifting between the two worlds. Her world was like a kaleidoscope, always changing patterns. Tess gently stroked the amiable dragon, while they waited at the psychiatrist's clinic. Mother crossed her fingers, desperately hoping this doctor could cure Tess's hallucinations.

The Mysterious Globe

It was Ari's Birthday. She didn't have a family. She grew up in foster homes, which she loathed. She graduated without any friends. So, when she got a courier, she didn't know who could have sent it to her.

She searched for the sender's name, but the parcel had been sent anonymously. It was wrapped in a shimmering red paper. Did the sender know that red was her favorite color? Or was it merely a coincidence?

Goofy, her dog, was jumping around excitedly. She tore the paper to open the gift. It was a globe.

"What the hell! Am I a kid?" she exclaimed, confused and disappointed.

She left the globe on the table and walked over to the kitchen. She made instant noodles. It was her staple diet, for she didn't enjoy cooking.

Ari tossed a bone towards Goofy, before attacking her noodles. That's when she noticed something in her peripheral vision. She jumped from her chair and ran to the table. The globe appeared different. The continents were not in their proper places. It puzzled her. She was sure they had been properly placed when she first looked at it.

She realized that this globe now had all the continents together, like Gondwana Land. She touched it – she could move the continents around.

“Fascinating!” she mumbled.

It was like a jigsaw puzzle. She could rearrange the pieces and make her own map – that she knew. She had never seen anything like it, before. She extracted the pieces one by one. The pieces weren’t made of paper or cardboard, but of some slimy substance. These pieces changed colors to blue and green when placed correctly, and became ebony otherwise.

When she touched the blue sea, she heard the sound of waves. She touched the green shades of forest and heard the rustling of leaves and distant calls of wild animals.

Mesmerized, she held her breath as she moved the continents. Before she could breathe, without any warning, she was sucked inside. The globe disappeared with her too.

Goofy could only see an unfinished bowl of noodles and a note on the floor, which read –

‘The Mysterious Globe – experience time travel.
Your destination is decided by your destiny’.

Neil's Shoes

Once again, it was Saturday. Neha dreaded this day, as it reminded her of her inadequacy as a doctor. She stepped into the storeroom. The room was dark, dingy, and dusty. It didn't belong to her neat and clean house. The bulb flickered ominously, when she turned on the light. She wanted to change the bulb and dust the objects, but it was too painful to be in this room.

The old and broken objects waited for her patiently. Every object had a story, every object held an intangible memory. She picked up a withered rose. The rose was one of the blissful memories she was proud of. The rose belonged to Vasu, who finally found a happier place. She always held the rose before touching any other object. It gave her hope, and motivated her to keep going.

Next, Neha picked up a pink scarf and wrapped it around her neck. Instantly, she found herself transported to a place with beautiful red and pink flowers all around. Zina was waiting for her.

"What took you so long?" Zina asked.

Neha didn't have the answer. She just smiled weakly.

Zina hugged her and said, "Look, Mother, I planted some flowers.

Aren't they beautiful?"

Neha held onto Zina and cried profusely, "Why did I let you go that day?"

Zina looked into Neha's eyes, "Because it was time, Mother. And it wasn't your fault."

They stayed talking about the things that mattered, and things that didn't. Zina was a precious child. Neha cried for days after Zina breathed her last. Zina's eyes always searched for her mother. Neha felt Zina's pain in her own heart. That's probably why she was the mother. Neha considered Zina to be her own child, a child she never had.

As Zina fell asleep, it was time for Neha to leave. She didn't want to go, but she knew the others were waiting too. She gave Zina an affectionate kiss and wrapped the scarf around her neck again. She was back in the storeroom. She felt lonely without Zina. Tears rolled down her cheeks.

Neha looked at the box of chocolates. She took the box in her hand and caressed it. Ranu loved to eat chocolates. Neha had got him a chocolate box and asked him to eat it when he recovered. He never recovered. The chocolates were all that was left.

She reached Ranu's space. It was quiet and warm. Ranu was delighted to see her, and happier to see the chocolates. He grabbed the unfinished chocolate box and munched on the sweet delicacies.

"Get me a different type next time," he spoke through a chocolate-stuffed mouth. "Yum, still so yum, Mother."

Ranu had the most innocent eyes. She blessed Ranu, and returned to the storeroom. A feeling of loneliness engulfed her.

Every week she would go to meet the kids, who she could not save at the hospital. She couldn't save them as a doctor, but she could be with them as their mother, until they finally left for a happier place. Perhaps that's why they all called her mother. It was her bizarre destiny - to comfort those kids until their liberation.

Next, Neha picked up a timeworn, torn brown shoe. The broken aglet used to be pristinely white, but now appeared yellowish brown. It belonged to Neil. She hesitated for a moment, for it was their first meeting. The first meetings were always arduous. Sometimes they didn't know that they had departed; sometimes they still wanted to hang on to the mortal world, and wanted to return. She didn't know how he would react. She picked up the shoes and some candies too. Most of the time, candies helped.

The place was too dark for her to see anything. It was frigid, so Neha decided to get a warm blanket the next time. She heard the rustling of the leaves and followed the sound. She spotted him under a tree, holding his face in his hand. He looked up, sensing her presence. Neil's perplexed look told her he had questions – they always did, the first time.

He didn't recognize her. She reminded him, "I was your doctor."

Slowly, the sorrow in his eyes gave way to anger.

"You could have saved me," Neil roared.

"Why didn't you save me? Because I was poor? An orphan? An invalid? I didn't have money to pay for the operation. Is that why?" he accused her.

"No, Neil…" she tried to explain.

"Yes, that's exactly what it was. My parents left me to die in the orphanage. You also let me die. And I trusted you as my mother!" he interrupted, angrily, and then he disappeared.

Neha waited for him to reappear, but he didn't. She found some candles around. She lit the candles. Perhaps he needed more time, she thought. She picked up the shoes to leave. The wind blew the candles as she left.

She returned to the storeroom, not realizing that she wasn't alone this time.

Dazzled

I see her sitting in front of me, her legs tense, her body stiff. The masseur in me yearns to lie her down on the bench. While I am having my random masseur fantasy (purely platonic), I notice the book that she is holding – ***Butterfly Skin*** by Se...

It's a pain to travel in the metro. You can't even read two words without being shaken to the core. Urgh! How is she able to hold that stare for so long? The book seems to grip her. I see something falling out of the book.. a ticket probably. The lady in the red skirt doesn't pay any attention. Her red dress is the perfect texture, rubbing against her perfect skin. Not like the porcupine men I have to massage every day.

The train comes to a halt. Few passengers get off and some get in. I too alight, only to re-enter from the other door and slide just next to her. Oh, boy! She smells so good. She looks at me. Can she read minds? No, relax, she can't.

She smiles. What's that phrase? *This smile can sail a boat*, or is it, *The smile can launch a thousand ships*? I smile back. She looks ethereal in the red skirt. I notice a butterfly on her shoulder. The wings are spread, as if the butterfly is ready to fly. The colorful tattoo adds to her enigma. I have never felt so attracted to anybody. Her skin looks so soft and velvety. I love the floral scented perfume she is wearing. Is it her enigma or her fragrance that intoxicates me?

“What happened?” she asks.

“Sorry?” I reply getting closer to her.

“What happened? You were sitting there, right?” she’s got me.

“Oh yeah! I was,” I stammer. “I just wanted to sit here.”

“Why?” she persists. A tough nut. Isn't she something?

“Just to see–” I am about to say 'you', when I realize she thinks I am talking about the view.

“Oh, I see. Are you new here?” she asks, in the most mellifluous voice I have ever heard. How I wish to keep listening to her always!

“Yes,” I lie.

“Do you want me to show you around? I am a local,” she offers biting her lips.

“Absolutely,” I answer. The train stops, and I follow her out.

The train comes to halt at the last stop. Every passenger alights. The ticket lying on the floor reads,

“The butterfly lady dazzled the masseur – he was trapped.”

Killer

Tanya, Kabir, John, and Rudra all stood perplexed.

Agent Roy walked around warning them, "You all are walking on a thin line here."

They looked at the body of the girl lying on the floor. There was blood on her face and wrist. The murder weapon was right there, next to the body. Agent Roy examined the knife without touching it. An impatient man of action, he wanted to solve this case on the spot. He knew that most of the killers did not leave fingerprints on the murder weapon, or at the crime scene. At least not since police procedurals had become popular on television.

Tanya looked pale. Maya and she were best friends. They loved to shop together, learned cooking together, even dreamt of marrying the same guy to stay together forever. Tanya was experiencing a myriad of feelings. There had been times when she was jealous of Maya. She had to be honest, at least with herself. She was somewhat relieved, for Maya was usually the center of attention. Now she could marry whoever she wanted. She looked at Kabir, who looked paler than her. But then, he always looked pale.

Kabir liked Maya a lot. But, she preferred John for company, and they were a couple. Kabir had devious plans to get them to break up. He had tried time and again, but he never succeeded.

He was sure everyone would suspect him, given his history. But didn't they know that he could never hurt Maya? Even while she lay on the floor, motionless, she looked so pretty. He looked at John, and wondered, '*How could he be so calm, his girlfriend just died!*'

John didn't know how to react. As Maya's boyfriend, he knew he would be the prime suspect. He was happy with her. However, of late, Maya was spending more time with Rudra. Tanya had been making advances on John. He was trying to appear calm. Working in theater helped him appear cool, even when a storm was raging inside him.

Rudra was standing in the corner, trying to hide his smile. But, his crooked tooth betrayed him, and showed up behind his otherwise sealed lips. He was a nerd, with little compassion. Maya and Rudra were friends and she had been telling him everything that was going on in her life. He knew everyone's secrets and what each of them was capable of.

Something about Kabir caught Agent Roy's attention.

"The color has drained from your face," the detective observed. "Kabir? Is it?"

Kabir nodded. He didn't trust his own voice.

"Where were you when it happened?" the detective interrogated.

"I was around here, we all were," stammered Kabir.

"Aha! So you know when it happened?" the detective almost shouted in triumph.

"Not exactly," Kabir seemed more confident now. "Sometime in the last hour."

"Did she look happy?" Roy questioned.

"She seemed quite happy when she opened the door. It's her birthday after all," Kabir replied.

"Then what happened?" the detective cleared his throat.

"I wished her and gave her a birthday present–" Kabir was stopped mid-sentence.

"Where is the birthday present?" Agent Roy badgered.

"Maya took it and left the room. I don't know where she kept it…" Kabir said.

The agent interrupted again, "Let's go and find it. Shall we?"

They all went to Maya's bedroom. Everything was scattered around the room.

"Oh my God! It's a burglary!" John exclaimed.

"Actually, no! Maya was not an organized person, this is how she liked to live. She thought the room looked more 'lively' this way," Tanya explained using airquotes.

"Still, we need to find out if anything valuable was stolen," Agent Roy declared.

They looked in the cupboard. They found her jewelry intact in the locker and the cash untouched.

"It's not a burglary. The killer was interested in something else," Agent Roy announced.

The agent walked to the table where all the gifts were kept neatly. There were four, one from each guest, except for Rudra.

The detective turned to Rudra, "What did you give her, Rudra?"

"I got her books. She loved to read," Rudra said.

"No, she didn't. She never liked to read," Tanya countered.

The detective's face lit up. At that moment, he thought he knew who the killer was.

Agent Roy turned towards Rudra. "You killed her because she fought with you for not getting her a gift," he accused.

"That's preposterous! This agent is crazy. Who does that?" shouted Rudra.

"It was Tanya! Don't you see?" a voice reverberated in the room. Everyone rose to their feet with a start, as if they had all seen a ghost.

"She loves books and has OCD. Look at the room, only the gifts are stacked neatly, and the books are missing. She saw the books and tried to steal them. She was caught, so she murdered her best friend."

"Argh!" everybody groaned in unison.

"You spoilt the fun, Maya!" Agent Roy scowled.

"C'mon! I got tired of playing dead on my own birthday. You guys were taking forever. It would be most inappropriate to die of hunger, whilst playing dead on my birthday. Now let's cut the cake," Maya licked the ketchup off her fingers.

Her other teenage friends followed her. Their whodunit party was fun as always.

Murder in the Palace

Amidst the lightning and thunder, a lone silhouette hurried along the vacant street. It was of a woman on a mission. An ominous bolt of thunder marked her arrival at the palace gates.

Ahana Roy looked up at the imposing structure shining brightly in the moonlight. The Mahal shimmered as if it was made of ice. She took a moment to appreciate the dazzling beauty of the handmade sculptures adorning the walls. She wished she were here under different circumstances. As she stepped up to the door, a feeling of sadness engulfed her. The palace didn't deserve a morbid story.

The teak gate stood ajar. Without any hesitation, Ahana stepped into the foyer. She hadn't noticed how wet she was, until her rain-soaked off-shoulder yellow dress, dripped a puddle on to the floor.

Few people can pull off a bedraggled look, but Ahana exuded confidence, and heads turned as she entered the parlor. A woman of poise, she carried herself with elegance. Except for one curvy ringlet on her forehead, her long, lustrous hair cascaded down her back.

Seeing Inspector Salim talking to one of the constables, she mumbled a quick greeting. Salim nodded in response, silently giving her the permission to carry on with her business. A detective by profession, Ahana was always prepared to tackle a case – she fished out a pair of latex gloves from her handbag. Her eyes wandered to the dead body on the floor.

"Not a good omen for the new year," she observed.

Ahana had been at a new year's party a few blocks away when she got a frantic call from her assistant, Bobby. Inspector Salim had been trying to reach her for a while. But the loud music had drowned out the sound of her cell phone ringing. Since the crime scene was just a few blocks away, Ahana had decided to walk down.

Ahana bent down to examine the body. The blood around the stab wound was fresh, she noted. She scanned the area around the body of the dead woman. Her trained mind noticed all the minute details, and she automatically committed them to memory. Near the body, a feather mask lay on the floor. It had been a masquerade party. A blood-soaked white rose lay next to the victim's fingertips. The victim, Sunaina Devi, was a forty-nine-year-old royal heiress with a reputation for being cantankerous.

Ahana looked around at the guests, or the pool of suspects, as she thought of them. She knew that the murder, though distressing, wasn't terribly shocking to most of the guests. Sunaina Devi had her fair share of enemies and then some. Ahana wondered who among the guests might benefit from this murder, and how.

Bobby had arrived some time before Ahana. He was dressed casually in wrinkled stonewashed jeans, in stark contrast to Ahana's personal style. But she didn't care about his scruffy appearance. She knew he was efficient, thorough, dedicated to his job, and that was all that mattered to her. She signaled for Bobby to follow her to the study, so she could find out what Bobby had learned.

As Ahana pulled up a chair, Bobby outlined the facts in his usual methodical style, "I got a call from Inspector Salim after midnight. I reached here in fifteen minutes and called you soon after. I have inspected the crime scene and questioned some of the suspects.

"Sunaina hosted a party every new year's eve. But this year, the party was more lavish, because she was celebrating the success of her debut music album."

"Oh yeah," interrupted Ahana, "I remember that album playing on my car radio a few times. Go on."

"After talking to various people, I have narrowed down the list of suspects to five people, including her current husband, Ranveer. Mr. Ranveer Dhilon and Sunaina Devi have been married for five years. He was her second husband, and she was his third wife. According to the servants, Ranveer and Sunaina often fought. In fact, she had asked for a divorce in front of Bhansingh, their *khansama*[1].

1. *Khansama – male cook, steward*

"In my opinion, Mr. Dhilon would have the most to gain from her death. Not only would he not need to pay any alimony, but he would also inherit the property and all the other assets she owned. Her death would be very convenient for Mr. Dhilon."

Even though Bobby was able to rattle off facts from memory like a machine, he needed to pause to breathe. Ahana gestured for him to continue, so Bobby resumed the narrative.

"Next, we have Mr. Akash Barnwal, who is the victim's ex-husband. They were married for 10 years, and then one day, Sunaina kicked him out of the palace and her life. I don't know why, but after that, Akash became destitute. Certainly, he was not happy with the situation. Several guests have confirmed that he gate-crashed the party. That leads me to suspect that he had an ulterior motive for being here. I haven't spoken to him yet. I thought, perhaps, you may want to do that first."

Ahana nodded thoughtfully, "Yes, you are probably right. What about others?"

Bobby leafed through his notes and continued. "Mr. Dhruv Sehgal is our third suspect. He was Sunaina's art dealer. I have heard some whispers about them having an affair. Dhruv could have a motive."

"Hmm. That's interesting," Ahana interrupted. "I'd better talk to Dhruv tonight too. Anyway, continue."

Bobby resumed, "Mrs. Padmini Sehgal was Sunaina's friend. She is

Akash's sister and Dhruv's wife. Padmini and Sunaina used to be close, but things between them turned sour due to the alleged affair between Dhruv and Sunaina."

Ahana's eyebrows shot up, "She seems to be entangled with quite a few people, doesn't she?"

Bobby nodded and continued, "The last suspect is Princess Amita Kumari, Sunaina's best friend. They often fought over trivial issues. A recent tabloid story mentioned that Amita was jealous of Sunaina's wealth, fame and success. At an interview last week, Amita accused Sunaina of stealing her song."

Ahana sighed. *It was not going to be easy to find the murderer when there were so many suspects with strong motives*, she mused.

"I'd better get started," she said to Bobby. "First Ranveer, then Dhruv," she rose from the chair and was surprised that the cushion was wet.

She had been so engrossed in the case that she had forgotten entirely about her rain-soaked dress. But now, with her attention drawn to it, she shivered and found it difficult to walk with the chiffon dress clinging to her legs. She decided to ask Ranveer for a change of clothes.

Ahana walked up to Ranveer and asked him to help her with a towel and some clothes. Relieved to leave the gruesome crime scene, Ranveer hurried towards the bedroom. Ahana walked with him.

Ranveer was a middle-aged man. He towered over Ahana by about a foot. Ahana couldn't help but notice the absence of bloodstains on his tuxedo. Clearly, he hadn't hugged and cried over his wife's dead body.

"I'm sorry for your loss, Mr. Dhilon. She seemed like a lovely lady," Ahana prompted, taking advantage of their isolation.

"She was, indeed. People often misunderstood her. She was gentle at heart, but often came across as raucous," said Ranveer, but his sympathetic words did not match his indifferent tone.

"She had many enemies. Half the people in this room hated her," he added, stealing a furtive glance at Ahana.

Ahana raised her eyebrows. "But not you?" she asked.

"Err... Not me. No. I loved her. She was my wife," he replied.

"Your third wife," Ahana pointed out.

"Yes, she was my third wife. My first wife succumbed to cancer. I loved her dearly. My second wife was a bitch. She ran away with some loser. I met Sunaina at a party. Isn't it ironic that we parted at a party too?" he asked philosophically.

"Murdered," Ahana corrected. "Your wife was just murdered, and you are professing your love for your first wife?" Ahana pursued.

"Here we are..." Ranveer declared, and Ahana realized that they had reached the bedroom. She waited for him to say something.

He gave her a towel and opened his wife's closet.

"Take your pick," he gesticulated to present the fabulous choices the wardrobe offered.

"Not that it will fit, but I am sure you will find something suitable." His eyes lingered for a moment on Ahana's bare shoulders before he hurried away under her sharp gaze. *No, he doesn't seem to be mourning his wife's death*, Ahana said to herself after he left.

Ahana rubbed her head vigorously with the towel and walked into the spacious closet. Sunaina wasn't fat by a long shot, but she wasn't as petite as Ahana either. Ahana took out a red dress. She felt weird trying on the clothes of a woman who had died merely an hour ago. She pulled out a matching, red leather jacket. It fit her well enough.

Out of habit, Ahana thrust her hands into the pockets of the jacket. There was something in there, a piece of paper, perhaps. Her curiosity piqued, Ahana took it out to examine it. It was a page from a diary, but the writing wasn't legible. Something to look in to later, she decided as she stuffed it back into the pocket and stepped out of the bedroom.

Ahana came to the top of the stairs. As she looked down, she appreciated the bird's-eye view of the gathering in the hall below. Most of the guests looked sad, some pretended to be, and the rest were pathetic actors. She tried to analyze the guilt and fear in their eyes. Everyone looked scared, but no one looked guilty. She knew she would soon have to let everyone go, but first, she wanted to speak to Dhruv Sehgal.

Ahana realized that cracking the case was going to take much longer than she had anticipated. She liked to solve a case when it was hot. She maintained that a case screamed when it was fresh, and the sound weakened or got lost in the noise, with every passing day.

Ahana made her way back to the study. Bobby was waiting for her.

"Send Dhruv, please," she said wearily as she plonked down on a chair with a dry cushion.

When Dhruv entered the room, Ahana addressed him, "Mr. Sehgal."

"Ms. Roy," he bowed.

She approved of chivalrous men. She noticed his immaculate dressing style. His custom-made suit complemented his toned, muscular body. His husky voice added enigma to his personality.

"What was the nature of your relationship with Sunaina Devi?" Ahana chose her words carefully.

"We were friends," Dhruv said, simply.

"Of course, you were. Anything else?" she probed.

"She was my client," he added tersely.

"And?" she coaxed.

An irritated frown crossed Dhruv's face. "And... as you... your assistant must have told you, we had a fling," he finally blurted out.

"A fling, you say? Nothing serious?" she persisted, much to Dhruv's chagrin.

"It's complicated," he was evasive.

"It always is. I am all ears," Ahana said, making herself comfortable on the chair.

Reluctantly, Dhruv launched into a long tale. "I always admired her for being the strong woman she was. A year ago, she hired me as her art dealer. She was a collector, and she was rich. We visited various parts of the world together, collecting rare, exotic paintings and sculptures. We discussed art and enjoyed each other's company," Dhruv paused.

"Go on," Ahana prompted.

"One day, she mentioned her weekend plans at Naples. I offered to join her. Then, you know, one thing led to another. Ever since then, there was no looking back. We couldn't stay away from each other. There were days when she was unsure, and then there were days when I was unsure. Yes, we liked spending time with each other. Is that a crime?" he demanded.

"It's adultery. In many countries, it's a punishable criminal offense," she offered.

"Well, not in India. Not anymore. It can be grounds for divorce. Nothing more," he retorted, and Ahana knew he was right.

"Your wife never objected?" Ahana asked, hoping this new avenue would lead somewhere.

"My wife..." Dhruv paused with a faraway look in his eyes. "Yes, she did. I explained there wasn't much to it," he added nonchalantly.

"So, you lied," Ahana pointed out.

He shrugged.

Dhruv obviously had no compunctions about lying, and Ahana was certain he hadn't been entirely truthful with her. She considered him to be her primary suspect. Calling their affair just a fling, gave Ahana a reason to doubt him, although he did seem genuinely infatuated by Sunaina.

"What is your profession, Mr. Sehgal?" Ahana asked, hoping to learn more about Dhruv.

"I am an art dealer. I buy paintings and art for my clients," he explained.

"Did Sunaina buy this from you?" Ahana gestured at the painting on the wall.

"She did. Last month," he looked tired.

"And how much did it cost?" she asked.

"Around USD 10,000," he answered, looking at his watch.

"Okay, Mr. Sehgal. That is all for now," she dismissed him. She had more questions. But this wasn't the time or the place. She knew she would not get more out of him tonight, while his defences were up. So she let him go.

She looked at the time. It was 3 o'clock. She asked Bobby to note down everybody's name, phone number, address, and Aadhar card number. She told them not to leave town, and she informed them that she might summon or visit them at any time of the day. Salim sent the body for a post-mortem. The palace was declared a crime scene. It was closed off to all, except the police, the forensic teams and the detective. Mr. Dhilon was asked to move to a hotel or stay with a friend or relative.

Ahana reached home, tired. Still in Sunaina's ill-fit red dress, she turned off the lights and collapsed on her bed. Yet, sleep eluded her.

She understood what Sunaina saw in Dhruv. Ahana found Dhruv chivalrous, charming, and intelligent. Ranveer, on the other hand, seemed relieved that Sunaina was no more. He professed his love for her, and yet he didn't shed tears. Then, he spoke of how he loved his first wife.

Ahana turned on the light again and picked up her diary. Writing down her thoughts helped her organize them, and stopped the buzzing in her mind. She opened her journal and scribbled away.

***

In the morning, Ahana drove to the palace. Smartly dressed in sleek black trousers and a crisp white shirt, she alighted from her car just outside the palace gates.

"Hello, boys!" she waved, flashing a dazzling smile at the police constables, as she strode past them. As if dazzled, they completely forgot to ask her for identification.

Ahana crossed the yellow tape and entered the palace. Bobby was already there. The chalk outline reminded her of the body lying on the floor the previous night. She asked a forensic expert about the fingerprints analysis report and the murder weapon. The expert told her that there was no sign of the murder weapon, and the fingerprint analysis would take a couple of days.

Ahana never relied on forensics. She believed that killers usually knew better than to leave their fingerprints at the crime scene. So, if perchance, any fingerprints were found, they often belonged to someone innocent. On the other hand, at a party, a killer would not be stupid enough to conceal their fingerprints, for they would be drowned in the sea of fingerprints belonging to the guests. In fact, any guest whose fingerprints did not show up would attract suspicion.

As six forensic experts were busily collecting fingerprints from every nook and cranny of the palace, Ahana smirked at the futility of it all.

The killer was smart to choose the day of the party. It would be difficult to find the culprit in the chaos. She wondered if this was a premeditated murder. Expecting no help from the 'expert team', she asked Bobby to obtain the call records of the deceased and all the five suspects.

She reached Sunaina's bedroom and went straight to the closet that she had walked into the night before. She looked through each drawer and cabinet, shoving important stuff into the black evidence box, while Bobby documented it all. Then she proceeded to check the pockets of trousers, dresses, and jackets. She found several receipts for concerts and plays. On rummaging through Ranveer's clothes and cabinets, she found several bills and concert tickets.

Next, Ahana turned her attention to the night-stand beside the bed. She opened the drawer in the nightstand, and there, in a secret compartment, she finally found what she was looking for – the Diary that once hosted the torn page she had found in the pocket of Sunaina's red jacket. She slid it into her purse, without telling Bobby and then glanced through the evidence collected in the black box. Ahana noted that the bills in

Ranveer's pockets were of purchases made by Sunaina. The tickets he had were for the same concerts that she had visited, but she observed that the seats were not next to each other. There were enough receipts for her to deduce that Ranveer was keeping a close watch on his wife.

Ahana concluded that Ranveer was aware of Sunaina's affair with Dhruv. She searched for more clues to strengthen her case. Just then, her eyes fell upon a most illuminating document. She beamed as she turned to Bobby and said, "I must see Mr. Dhilon."

Wasting no time, Ahana left for the hotel, where Mr. Dhilon had checked in the previous night.

It was afternoon by the time she reached the hotel. She walked to the reception, showed her badge, and asked for Mr. Dhilon's room. The receptionist promptly obliged her with the room number and directions.

Ahana walked up to the door and rang the bell. Mr. Dhilon opened the door with a smile on his face and a glass in his hands.

"Mr. Dhilon, were you expecting me?" she asked.

"Indeed, I was. But I almost forgot how beautiful you are," Ranveer tried flirting.

"Mr. Dhilon, had I not known that your wife passed away yesterday, I would have assumed you are celebrating," Ahana said, stepping into the room.

"Well, I am. I'm celebrating my freedom. Do you want to join the celebrations?" he asked, gesturing towards the champagne bottle.

"Sure," she accepted the offer, hoping that the alcohol would loosen his tongue. She perched daintily on the red couch next to Ranveer.

"So tell me, Mr. Dhilon," she began, sipping her chilled champagne.

"Tell you what? Let's drop the formalities, Ahana. Call me Ranveer,"

Ahana smiled, "Okay! Ranveer, tell me. Yesterday, you professed your love for your dead wife, and today, you are celebrating her death. What does this mean?"

"Yesterday, she had just died, and I did love her. Then, last night, I wondered why I should mourn her death. She was having an affair with Dhruv, that bastard. Pardon my French, but they were having an affair right under my nose.

They thought I was blind. Well, I knew she was incapable of loyalty. I didn't care until the day she told me that she wanted a divorce. I didn't want to end up like Barnwal. So, I followed her around town. I needed to gather evidence of her extra-marital affair. She went with Dhruv to concerts and plays, and to other countries under the pretext of buying art. He loved her money," he hissed.

"Like you?" Ahana asked, amused.

"I like beauty with brains. Yes, like me, but I was her husband.

And I wasn't wasting her money the way he was. That stupid woman couldn't tell Picasso from Beethoven," he grumbled.

"Beethoven..." Ahana was puzzled.

"Exactly! She didn't even know Beethoven was not a painter, but a musician. She was spending millions of money on that bastard," Ranveer seethed.

"So you suspect Dhruv Sehgal," Ahana concluded.

"I suspect everyone. But mostly Sehgal and Barnwal. Do you know that Barnwal once attacked her in the middle of the road? That drunkard almost pushed her to her death. Had I not been there, she would have been dead right then," he paused to sip his drink.

"Why did he do that?" this was news to Ahana.

"You are smart enough to figure it out yourself, Ahana!" he smirked and challenged Ahana.

"Do you still love your first wife?" Ahana's tone softened.

"That doesn't have anything to do with the case, does it?" Ranveer replied.

"Please answer the question," she waited patiently.

"Yes. Maybe that, or perhaps we always build a romantic image of someone we lose to death. We romanticize the death of our loved ones," for once, Ranveer looked genuinely sad.

"You lost Sunaina to death too. So, why are you not romanticizing her death?" Ahana was relentless when it came to her job.

"We had fallen apart," Ranveer answered.

"Mr. Dhilon, I mean Ranveer, did she show you her new will?" Ahana asked.

Ranveer's eyes grew wide, and his cheeks flushed as he digested this new piece of information. He lost control and spilled a few drops of his bubbly beverage on his clothes, "What will? Where is it?" he shouted out in anger.

"I am sure you are smart enough to figure that out yourself," she winked.

"See you soon, Ranveer," Ahana put her glass on the table and left the room.

***

Ahana fell asleep in her library, hunched over her desk, amidst the evidence, her notes, and the yellow diary. Her subconscious mind must have been working on the problem. In the middle of the night, she woke up with a start.

She was sweating profusely, and she was famished. She remembered that she hadn't eaten anything before dozing off. She went to the kitchen for a drink of water. Remembering her task at hand, she splashed her face and made coffee instead. It was going to be a long night, and she needed to be alert.

With a steaming mug of coffee in her hand, she walked to the balcony for some fresh air.

"Ouch!" she exclaimed, as she stepped on something hard, spilling hot coffee on her clothes. She picked up the troublesome object. It was a stone wrapped with a piece of paper with something scribbled in red.

She placed her mug on a small table in the balcony and moved towards the light to read the note.

Ms. Roy,
stay away from the palace case or else...

Neither the red color nor the contents of the note, achieved their desired effect on Ahana. She kept the note in her cupboard without giving it a second thought and sipped her black coffee.

***

The next morning, Ahana went to Amita's house. She rang the bell, and promptly, Amita opened the door and invited her in. As Ahana walked in, her sharp eyes scanned the room and noted every detail. It was an old place. Amita offered Ahana some tea, which she politely declined.

Ahana would have never guessed about Amita's royal lineage, given her bohemian choice of attire. Her Balearic boho dress was too loose for her tiny frame. The jangle of her bangles and necklaces filled the room before Ahana asked her first question.

"I hear that you and Sunaina were best friends?" Ahana started.

"We were. We did everything together. We went to the movies, shopped, and traveled together. We were unicorn friends. I miss her. I can sense that she will come back to me at any moment now. She is still here; I can feel her presence. Can you feel her? Do you have any idea what it feels like? It's like, I can't even breathe properly. Can you breathe? Of course, you can. You haven't lost a friend. She was my cousin too," Amita blabbered on.

"I know, I know," Ahana patted Amita on her shoulder. "But did you two ever fight?"

"Yes. We did. All friends do, don't they?" she looked at Ahana for reassurance, and Ahana nodded, giving her hand a gentle squeeze.

Pleased with Ahana's sympathetic attitude, Amita continued,

"She changed, you know. After her success, she was like a different person. They say success goes to your head, and that's probably what it was with her. We wrote that song together, you know. The lyrics were mine."

"You say you wrote that song?" Ahana interjected.

"Yes, I wrote it and then shared it only with her. I have proof that I wrote the song. After finishing a song, I copy it on a piece of paper, seal it, and then mail it to myself. When I receive the mail, I don't open it. Instead, I keep it as a record. You can have a look, if you want, and crosscheck the dates. Yet, she never gave me any credit," Amita sounded bitter.

"Why didn't she give you credit?" Ahana inquired.

"I don't know. Last year, when she was frequently traveling to Europe with Dhruv, I went to New York on a long vacation to meet my sister. Actually, Sunaina sponsored the trip, or perhaps, she sent me there on purpose. When I returned, after more than a month, our song was already a hit. I confronted her, but she was evasive. She just acknowledged me as her inspiration. She never included me, even though she knew I was broke. I didn't have money for anything," Amita was on the verge of tears.

"What was going on between Dhruv and Sunaina?" Ahana asked, handing her a tissue.

Dabbing her eyes, Amita continued, "The world knows. The

young man charmed the old lady, probably for her money. They were going together all the time, and Ranveer didn't like it."

"What happened at the party?" Ahana pressed on.

"She threw a success party. I borrowed a dress from her. I didn't even have a goddamn dress. I loved her, I did. She called me to help her with the party. I was right there when it happened. The lights went off, moments before midnight. We were all counting, laughing, dancing, and clapping. The lights stayed off for a while. And then, we all heard a shriek. When the lights came back, she was dead. Her blood was all over the floor. Everybody started screaming; I stood frozen. Someone called the police. On Police's advice, immediately all the doors were closed, so nobody could escape," Amita elaborated.

"Do you suspect anyone?" Ahana asked.

Amita thought for a moment before replying, "No, I don't suspect anyone in particular. But I don't trust any of them."

Unicorn friends? Was this lady really crazy? She seemed quite smart. She was prudent enough to keep records of her compositions in a way that would serve as proof in a court of law. She even figured out that Sunaina sent her away, so she could claim full credit for the song. *Perhaps, she acts crazy, so that people don't take her too seriou*sly, Ahana mused. Ahana sympathized with Amita, but she couldn't exonerate her, not yet.

***

`Tread cautiously unless you're eager to join Sunaina Devi.`

Ahana received an email. These threats lacked originality, and they were getting quite tiresome. On the bright side, it meant that the culprit was scared, very scared.

Ahana called Bobby and asked him to summon Mr. Akash Barnwal, at his house.

When she reached Bobby's house, Akash was waiting for her in his alabaster colored t-shirt and blue jeans. His salt and pepper stubble made him appear older than he was.

“Hello, Ms. Roy. Do I have the honor of being at the top of your suspect list? Believe me, I didn't do anything to earn the privilege. I swear,” Akash ventured before Ahana could ask anything.

“Mr. Barnwal, please have a seat. You need not worry if you haven't done anything. So, calm down, and let's talk,” Ahana tried to put him at ease. “Would you care for some tea, or coffee perhaps?”

“Yes, please. Tea would be great and something to eat, please,” Akash replied, seating himself on the couch.

Ahana waited for Bobby to leave. Then, she sat down next to Akash and asked, “How did you become homeless?”

Akash sighed and proceeded to recite the tragic story of his life that no doubt gave him many a sleepless night, "Sunaina was a royal heiress. I was a businessman. My company imported beautiful carpets from around the world. It was going great until my largest client defaulted, after a fire in his showroom. A month later, I discovered that my accountant had been pocketing the money marked for taxes. Still, I could not gather sufficient proof to have him convicted. I fired him, but I already owed the government a considerable amount in unpaid taxes.

"Circumstances conspired against me. There was a dramatic decline in the price and the demand for my carpets, as new machine-woven, cheaper carpets became more popular. In no time, I was neck-deep in debt."

A note of bitterness crept into his voice as he continued, "I asked Sunaina for help. Not only did she refuse, but she also cleaned out a substantial sum in our joint account, which included some of my own hard-earned money. Clearing my debts left me penniless," he stopped to sip the tea Bobby had served. As soon as Bobby kept a plate of cookies on the table, Akash hurriedly ate the cookie, as if he hadn't eaten for days.

Akash leaned back on the couch, and he continued, "Our marriage was not going well, but I hoped to fix things. Then one day, out of the blue, she served me with divorce papers. She didn't think twice before throwing me out of her life, like a vestigial organ."

"Was that the reason you attacked her?" Ahana inquired.

"I don't remember attacking her. I was drunk. I don't remember any of it. I only know what she told me later," he explained.

"Did you love her?" Ahana asked.

"Yes, I loved her. It took me a long time to get over her. A part of me still loves her. I guess a part of me always will," Akash softly said.

Ahana felt sorry for the poor man. Fate had handed him a raw deal. But she must do her job, so she continued, although feeling a twinge of guilt at badgering a broken man.

"Why did you gate-crash the party?" she enquired.

"I did so because I wanted to talk to Sunaina. I had to warn her about someone," he answered.

"Who did you want to warn her about?" Ahana was curious.

"Dhruv Sehgal. I knew she wanted to divorce Ranveer and marry Dhruv. However, I had to warn her that he was not the right man for her," Akash looked dazed.

"And you chose the day of the party to warn her?" Ahana asked, her eyebrows raised.

He interrupted, "I didn't know she had a party. I learned about it only when I reached the palace that evening, and she asked me to stay for the party. Then she got busy with the guests, and I with my drinks."

"What do you know about Dhruv?" Ahana asked.

"That behind the charming exterior, Dhruv has a perilous side. His art business is a legal front for his illicit dealings with the mafia. I learned it from the horse's mouth – one of Dhruv's customers, who I met at a bar. Dhruv cannot be trusted. He may well be the murderer," Akash revealed.

Ahana needed time to process all this information. Her mind was in a whirl linking the new pieces of the puzzle, with threats she received through email, and the note wrapped in stone. The gears in her brain whirred, as all the pieces seemed to be falling together. But she needed more. Some crucial information was amiss.

***

Ahana called Mrs. Padmini Sehgal to check if Dhruv was home. When Padmini mentioned that Dhruv was out, Ahana decided to visit her right away.

When Ahana Roy reached the Sehgal residence, the door was ajar, so she peeped inside and called out, "Mrs. Sehgal?"

"Come inside, dear," Padmini sang out.

Feeling welcome, Ahana stepped inside the beautifully decorated parlor. Padmini was sitting comfortably on her recliner couch in her shamrock top and pine shorts. Her shoulder-length ebony hair suited her angular jawline. She greeted Ahana with a smile, which didn't reach her green eyes.

"How are you?" Ahana asked.

"I have seen better days, but I am alright," Padmini replied.

"You can start with your list of questions, dear," she added.

"What happened at the party?" Ahana began.

"We were all having fun. Everybody started dancing to Sunaina's song. We made a temporary stage, set up disco lights, and played the song in a loop. Sunaina was the first one to dance. She pushed me to go next. It was one crazy night. Friends and family gathered together to celebrate a special occasion.

"Dhruv was hilarious, with his adaptation of MJ – doing a moonwalk. We were in splits when the lights were turned off, moments before the New Year. Then we heard a shriek. After a few seconds, the lights were back on, and Sunaina lay on the floor, dripping blood," Padmini recalled.

"How was your relationship with Sunaina?" Ahana asked.

"Sunaina and I have been good friends since our college days. A lot of people considered her cantankerous, but I saw it as her idiosyncrasy. I didn't judge her for it. We were friends, and I accepted this aspect of her personality," Padmini answered.

"Despite her marriage getting sour with your brother, you were good friends?" Ahana was skeptical.

"It soured our relationship for some time. Initially, I was upset with Sunaina for what she did to Akash. But I knew her longer than he did and better than others. I knew that she had a good heart, but loyalty was not her strong suit... Anyway, since life moves on, I chose to help my brother in re-establishing his business, rather than being bitter about Sunaina. Over the years, I forgave her," Padmini explained.

"How was it going between the two of you in the recent past?" Ahana probed.

"Life was getting normal again. That was when I heard from Akash about Sunaina and Dhruv. I was not surprised since Dhruv himself had told me about meetings and some traveling with Sunaina related to business. It was only when others noticed their frequent meetings and told me, I was upset," Padmini answered.

"Why did you go to the party then?" Ahana questioned.

"I didn't want to. Dhruv made me," Padmini sulked.

"Hmm… Did you ever confront Sunaina about her affair with Dhruv?" Ahana pressed on.

"No, but I asked Dhruv. He assured me that it was nothing and that I had nothing to worry about," Padmini explained.

"And you believed him?" Ahana queried.

"I..." Padmini hesitated. "I had no proof to the contrary," Padmini conceded.

Ahana didn't have any more questions for Padmini. She thanked Padmini for her time and left.

As she drove, Ahana thought about all the suspects she had interrogated. Each one had a motive, but their stories seemed plausible. The trick was to figure out which one was lying.

***

Back at home, Ahana got a call from Karnal, the forensic expert. He informed her about traces of blood found in one of the washrooms, which matched Sunaina's. He also told her about a single, blood-stained, yellow sock found in the washroom drain pipe. The blood on the sock also matched Sunaina's. He tried to extract DNA from the sock, but no hair or skin was retrieved.

She asked him to attempt a touch DNA analysis. A simple act of picking up an object, or touching a surface, can lead to the identification and apprehension of a criminal. Karnal also told her what she already expected, the fingerprints were too numerous to be used as evidence.

Ahana asked Bobby to send handwriting samples of all the suspects to a handwriting expert, along with the threatening note that she had received. Bobby updated Ahana about his findings regarding the call records of the suspects. There was nothing suspicious, except a few calls made to a public phone booth by one of the suspects.

Ahana checked for the IP address of the threatening email, to determine its origin. She tracked the email, but her efforts were futile. The user had been smart enough to use a VPN service.

Ahana's head was throbbing from the mental effort she had expended over the last few days trying to connect the many dots the case presented. She decided to take a relaxing bath.

While the lukewarm water filled the bathtub, she lit scented candles and poured a glass of wine. She turned on some soft, soothing music, before adding bubble soap and lavender oil in the tub. As she luxuriated in the warm water, the muscles in her body relaxed. The wine and music helped her unwind. As soon as she closed her eyes, a eureka moment made her jump out of the tub. She pulled a towel, wrapped it around herself, and ran to her laptop.

She programmed a gif, added a message, *I'm waiting for your next move*, and dispatched it to the sender of the threatening email.

The gif was programmed to extract the IP address of the sender, if the VPN routing was turned off. Ahana knew it was a long shot, but it was worth a try. What had she to lose from it? She also called a cyber-cell to help her extract the actual IP address.

Satisfied with her little trick, Ahana returned to her paradise in the bathroom with a book.

Ahana looked for word-based clues as she believed that if suspects talked enough, they would inadvertently reveal their true nature through their words. Ahana also knew words could mislead, and smart criminals would often plant red herrings or an outright lie.

She knew it was important to give the suspects a chance to tell their stories with their truths and lies. This allowed her to understand the suspects and their reasons for lying.

Ahana sat with her files, documents, evidence, call records, and pages from her diary scattered on her bed. She knew there were some red-herrings.

So she examined all the facts methodically to search for inconsistencies. First, she summed up all the key evidence against each suspect.

Ranveer, the relieved widower:

1) He was not mourning his wife's death. He did not even bother to pretend anymore.

2) The color on his face drained when he learned about the new will. It appeared as if his plan had failed.

3) He was collecting proof of Sunaina's extramarital affair. Why? Perhaps, to get a better deal in the divorce.

4) He admitted that Sunaina wanted a divorce, in which case he would be a big loser.

Most of the evidence was against the smooth and charming Dhruv:

1) Everybody pointed their fingers at Dhruv.

2) Ahana had proof that Dhruv was scamming Sunaina in his art-dealings.

3) He had mafia-links

4) Sunaina's latest will named him as the sole beneficiary.

Padmini, Dhruv's wife, surprisingly forgiving of all of Sunaina's idiosyncrasies, as she called them:

1) She said that she forgave Sunaina, which Ahana doubted.

2) Ahana couldn't extract any reactions from Padmini about Dhruv and Sunaina. It almost seemed like she had rehearsed her answer to that question.

Destitute Amita, who had been cheated off her one sole shot at a fortune by Sunaina:

1) Her call records showed calls to a public booth, until the day of Sunaina's death, which was suspicious.

2) Amita was a dangerous combination of jealous and crazy.

Akash, an ex-husband irrationally in love, and a victim of circumstances, as well as of Sunaina's cruelty and selfishness:

1) He gate-crashed the party. No one else corroborated his claim that Sunaina wanted him to stay on.

2) He almost pushed Sunaina to death, which he claimed to have no recollection of.

3) Ahana had a strong suspicion that the calls Amita made to the public booth were to Akash.

***

The next morning Ahana checked her email. She had received a reply from the killer in the form of a gif that read, *'you are dead'.* She smiled. She was enjoying the game.

She called the cyber cell and gave them access to her email account, so they could nab the sender. The cyber cell informed her that they had not yet succeeded in obtaining the IP address of the previous email. The VPN service provider required written permission from the National Cyber Crime

Unit to disclose such private information. They also confirmed that her gif was opened using the VPN, so the IP address could not be extracted.

Ahana drove to Dhruv's house once more, this time to meet Dhruv himself.

She rang the bell, and Dhruv opened the door. He guided her to the living room.

"Everybody suspects you," Ahana said, without preamble.

"That doesn't make me a murderer, now, does it?" Dhruv asked.

"Why does everyone suspect you?" Ahana persisted.

"Maybe they are jealous. I am the only one who didn't feel victimized by her," Dhruv argued.

Ahana switched tracks, "What do you know about Amita and Akash?"

"Akash is my brother-in-law, but we don't get along. I believe he loved Sunaina a lot. I don't really know Amita, so I can't say anything about her. I suspect that Amita and Akash are seeing each other. Still, for whatever reason, they wanted to keep their relationship a secret," Ahana detected a hint of sarcasm in Dhruv's tone.

"What about Ranveer?" she interrogated.

"I don't understand him at all. Sunaina was really upset with him. He used to be busy in his own world. He was seeing other women. And he never trusted Sunaina," Dhruv replied.

"What do you have to say about the art collection you sold Sunaina?" Ahana observed Dhruv, as she asked this crucial question.

"What about it?" Dhruv retorted.

"Was it overpriced?" Ahana persisted.

"Sure. It was exorbitantly overpriced. It was business, and I was going to get as much as I could. I'm no sentimental fool. This still doesn't make me a murderer," Dhruv pointed out.

"It could be a strong motive. Maybe she got to know about it," Ahana ventured.

"Ms Roy, you are crossing the line. I have been cooperative so far. You are accusing me without any evidence. This counts as harassment. Next time we speak, it will be in the presence of my lawyer." With that, he got up and showed her the door.

"Fine. Tomorrow, be present at the palace at 10:00 a.m., with or without your lawyer – your choice," Ahana instructed, and left.

She called Bobby from her car. He was in the office with the party pictures from the day of the murder. She told Bobby to summon all the suspects at the palace at 10 o'clock the next morning.

When Ahana reached the office, Bobby had already organized all the information Ahana had asked for, on the table. She went straight to her laptop to check the pictures from the day of the murder.

She used her latest software to zoom in the pictures. In a few minutes, she found the yellow sock and its owner. The handwriting expert was also able to identify the writer of the threatening note. Now, the touch DNA report was all she was waiting for.

Her thoughts drifted to the threatening note she had received. Hot on the trail of the murderer, it amused her. *Let's see who's dead now*, she said to herself.

***

Ahana stood in the palace where it all began. She knew that the suspects would be reluctant to show up today. So, she had summoned them through Salim. Bobby informed Ahana about the arrival of the suspects. Apart from the inspector Salim, along with his two police officers inside the hall, a larger squad of policemen waited outside Mahal, ready to apprehend the killer, should he or she try to escape.

Ahana welcomed her guests, "I am glad you all came. Not coming would have clearly given you away. Now, let's get down to the business of unmasking the murderer. As you have probably guessed, the five of you were the prime suspects." She took a couple of steps towards Ranveer, who was seated closest to her.

"Ranveer, you looked very confident when I first met you. Not so confident today. Are you?" she observed.

Then, she turned her attention to Amita, "Amita, you pretended to be somebody you are not. Apparently, you like to hide your jealousy and treachery behind a pretence of madness."

Methodically she moved on to the next person. It happened to be Dhruv.

"Mr. Sehgal, as you know, everyone suspected you. Sunaina's latest will, drafted just a few days before her murder, named you the sole beneficiary of her estate. You claimed to be unaware of it, yet, you were clearly close. It's hard to believe that she didn't confide in you. You also seem to be the person who gains most from her death."

"Ms. Roy, as I told you before, none of this is evidence of me being a murderer," Dhruv sneered.

"Yes, Mr. Sehgal. You did point that out. So I went through the trouble of bringing this sock. It has Sunaina's blood on it, and it was shoved down the bathroom drainpipe. It is your sock, isn't it, Mr. Sehgal?" Ahana pulled out a picture from her pocket.

"Absurd, I did not do anything," said Dhruv. His expression soured.

"I know how much you value material evidence Mr. Sehgal, so I got more. Tell me, how do you explain the DNA touch report, which confirms the sock with Sunaina's blood strains over it belongs to you? The will, of course, is the biggest motive," Ahana charged.

"Motive, means and opportunity, you had them all, and the physical evidence all points to you. Arrest him, officer, he is the murderer!" she declared, dramatically pointing a finger at Dhruv.

"No! He didn't! He didn't do it! You don't know what you are talking about," Padmini broke down. "It was me, he was just trying to save me." Padmini confessed.

She spoke between sobs, "It was my plan. I made him go after Sunaina, and sell her art at exorbitant prices, so I could use the money to help Akash in his business. But Sunaina and Dhruv fell for each other. I didn't see that coming. I asked Dhruv about it. He skirted the issue by telling me that he was doing only what I had asked of him."

Padmini's eyes became feverish, and her voice trembled. She looked directly at Dhruv as she spoke, "On that fateful evening, just before midnight, I didn't see Sunaina or Dhruv around. I went to look for them, and found them making out in the guest room. Seeing them together made my skin crawl. The sight of Dhruv with another woman made my blood boil, and I lost it," Padmini stood up and screeched out in agony, as if she were reliving the terrible moment.

Then, exhausted, she sat back down.

Her shoulders slumped, as she continued, "I got the meat knife from the dining table and went back to the room. They saw me and sprang to their feet. Before either of them could react, I stabbed the knife right through her heart. She couldn't even scream. While falling, she held Dhruv's foot. She wanted to say something, but died on the spot," Padmini said matter-of-factly.

Emotionally spent, she continued speaking tonelessly, "Dhruv was shocked, and I froze. He decided to help me. Perhaps he still loved me and didn't want me to go to jail. As luck would have it, just then the living room lights were turned off to usher in the New Year. While people were still dancing, I quickly washed the knife and placed it back on the dining table. Dhruv stuffed his bloody sock down the drain. When I came out, nobody was around. I shrieked in Sunaina's voice. The lights came back in a few seconds."

Padmini seemed relieved to get it all off her chest.

"I didn't want to kill her," Padmini looked around, wondering if anyone believed her.

When she received no sympathetic looks or words, she shrugged,

"I couldn't bear to see her stealing my husband. She had already ruined my brother's life. There was a limit to how much betrayal I could take. That note and the email were sent by me to mislead you. Dhruv is innocent." Padmini concluded, and looked around, wondering what would happen next.

Ahana smiled, "I knew that you were the mastermind, but he isn't innocent either. After arriving here on the night of the murder, I had to use Sunaina's jacket. In a pocket of the jacket, I found a crumpled paper. It was from Sunaina's diary with something illegible scribbled on it. I learned that she must have a diary. Next morning, when I came to the palace, I found the diary. From it, I learned what she thought about you all," Ahana paused to examine the expressions on the faces of various members of her audience, before she continued.

"She was remorseful about taking credit for Amita's song and decided to leave the other house to her. She also wrote about Padmini confronting her after the Paris trip with Dhruv. When I asked Padmini, she lied that she had never confronted Sunaina, which made me suspicious. The new will, which I found in Sunaina's drawer, and the entries in her diary, made it clear to me that Dhruv could not be the culprit," Ahana was satisfied to see Amita and Dhruv gaping at her in surprise.

Revealing startling facts, and studying people's reactions, was the part of being a detective, she most enjoyed. Unable to contain her excitement as she approached the climax, Ahana stood up and paced.

"When the IP address revealed the Sehgal address, it wasn't

difficult to find out who the culprit was. All the evidence was against Dhruv and none against Padmini. Left with no other option, I needed Padmini's public confession. That's why I called you all here, today," she concluded flourishing her arms.

Padmini was taken into police custody. Dhruv too was taken into custody for aiding and abetting the murderer, or merely, covering for his wife.

Fifty Shades of Pink

June 25, 2018

The musical rain and the rustling leaves enhanced the mystique of the midnight hours. The silhouettes of trees danced to the symphony of nature. The rain gods showered the city with their blessings.

Kira finally left the warmth of her bed, after staring out of the window, hypnotized by the sight outside for over an hour. Plagued by insomnia, she hoped to find solace in a midnight cup of coffee.

Kira hummed as she sashayed to the kitchen. While the coffee was brewing, she looked out of the window. The rain reminded her of something, and just like that, alone in her flat, at midnight, she started laughing hysterically.

As if on cue, the phone rang. She answered the call. It was her best friend, Sheeba.

"Hey, buds!" Kira greeted her.

"Hi, Kira," Sheeba chirped.

"You won't believe it. I was just thinking about you guys. It's raining here in Mumbai. It reminded me of the day we met Daniel for the first time… that scarf… it was instrumental in getting you guys together."

"Yeah, you know what? He still doesn't let me buy any shade of pink."

July 11, 2015

Kira, Sheeba, and Ally landed in Goa and headed for the hotel. It was already getting dark by the time they had checked in. They decided to leave in an hour and told the concierge to arrange for a rented car.

When they arrived at the reception desk at 8 pm, ready for the evening, the boy from the rental car company was already waiting for them. He handed over the car keys to the girls and gave them the standard briefing. Kira lapped up the keys and jumped to the steering wheel.

It was a pleasant evening. As they drove down the serpentine roads, it started drizzling. They rolled down the windows and drank in the petrichor that wafted in with the cool breeze. All of a sudden, they heard a thumping sound.

"Oh my God! There isn't a tire repair shop in sight. What are we going to do?" Sheeba, the scaredy cat panicked. The girls inspected the tires but they seemed fine.

"Genius!" Ally sneered, "How do we know which one is flat?"

And they heard it again, "Thud thud thud." This time, they could tell that the sound was coming from the boot. They were scared, and to make things worse, it started pouring harder. Frightened, they held on to each other, and somehow managed to open the boot.

Sheeba shrieked when she saw a man in the boot. But their fear vanished, when they looked carefully. All three girls burst out laughing. A man in his twenties, stark naked, hiding his manhood with his left hand, stepped out of the trunk. He shivered in the cold rain. The girls laughed, while the poor guy stood embarrassed in the middle of the road.

Finally, recovering from her giggling fit, Sheeba felt sorry for the naked stranger and handed him her scarf. The three girls turned the other way, overcome by a fresh wave of giggles.

The stranger took a moment to cover himself, while the girls tried in vain to compose themselves.

"Thanks for the scarf," the guy said.

The girls turned around. The guy was standing with a pink scarf tied to his waist, the colour of his cheeks matching the scarf. In between the guffaws, they asked him who he was, and what was he doing inside the boot, naked.

"I'm Daniel. I came to Goa with my friends. We rented this car for two days, and yesterday, we all were out till the wee hours of the morning at LPK. Now, I find myself here, in the boot of car we rented."

Daniel pressed his fingers against his temples. "Oh! My head hurts," he groaned.

"Where are my friends? Oh no! Did my friends return the car, leaving me in the boot? How could they? I don't know how and when I got in the boot. The last thing I remember, is the rounds of shots we had before leaving LPK."

"We are Sheeba, Kira, and Ally. Do you want us to drop you somewhere?" Sheeba managed to say between gasps of laughter.

"Yeah. For now, do you guys have anything that I can wear?" Daniel asked, miserably looking at the scarf.

Ally pulled out a pink sweatshirt from her bag and a towel. Daniel wore the pink sweatshirt, and wrapped the towel around his waist.

The sweatshirt was a little tight, but Daniel didn't have a choice. He thanked the girls. As they started the car, Ally said, "O boy! We just witnessed 50 shades of pink." The girls burst into another fit of giggles.

The Time Traveller

In my era, people were peace lovers. They revered *Anviya**, Gandhi, Mandela, Mother Teresa. All I ever heard was Gandhi said this, Teresa did that. The nagging reminders to 'be good, be kind' were nauseating. They painted a rosy picture of peace loving heroes and left out the thorns. Not only was this 'perfect' utopian society a sham, it was also incredibly boring!

As a time traveller, I had met many famous personalities – from Gandhi to Hitler, Alexander to Da Vinci. These icons were nothing like their one-dimensional caricatures disgracing the pages of the history books.

The weapons of mass destruction had been unleashed several times during World War-4. As a result, the planet had turned into a desert. Only the elite, a select few with access to the secret bunkers, had survived. These bunkers had been built strategically, all around the globe.

The world wasn't divided anymore. There was no language, country, religion or money to divide humans. All that people of my era wanted was to save humanity and earth.

But there was a catch. We had the resources to survive for only another thousand years. Our only hope was to find a habitable planet, and that's where we directed all our efforts and energy.

We successfully pushed the average mortality age to 160 years, but it wasn't like we would live to see the end of the earth. How long can you sing one song of peace? How I wished I could do something to bring back the conflicts that once divided us.

Year: 2000
Place: Las Vegas, The Sin City

Vegas was my favorite place to be. It had everything I craved for: alcohol, gambling, meaningless sex, sumptuous food, and drama. Somehow, it was easier to hear myself think amidst the indistinct chatter in a crowded place, than in my own quiet era. I wished I could stay here forever.

Unfortunately, there were some rules for time travellers. One rule was that we could only stay for a few days. Besides, time travel caused severe headaches. Medications were available, but they were rationed and monitored by scrupulous officers. I was told to keep myself hydrated while traveling through time, sage advice which I never followed, and usually, upon returning, I paid for my stubbornness with a severe migraine.

I gulped down the charred octopus with a potent cocktail and turned to the bartender.

"Pour me another drink, bartender," I demanded, pointing at

the empty glass.

"Where are you from?" he asked, eyeing me suspiciously, as if I were from another planet. He couldn't be more wrong.

I should have lied, but my only character flaw - I could never lie. So I twisted the truth, told the half-truth, hid the truth... but I never lied.

"What's your name, bartender?" I asked, instead of replying.

"Call me D. What's yours?" staring at my devilishly handsome face, he asked.

"I'm Arch. I'm from here... somewhere," I answered, randomly pointing around. Given his profession, I guessed he was used to vague answers.

Flipping the lid of the flask, he poured me a drink. I swallowed it in a jiffy and slammed the glass down.

"Check, please," I called out, extracting a heavy wallet.

Being a collector, I always had money for anywhere and anytime. Though strictly forbidden in my era, I smuggled currencies from around the world. The game kept me alive, the only spark of excitement in my oppressively monotonous life.

Sometimes, I did crazy things for laughs. Once I dressed a mummy in Adidas shoes. Placing a Swiss watch in an old coffin was exciting. I even played a clueless time traveller from Taured. What fun!

As I handed the cash to the bartender, I noticed him rub his face in exasperation.

"This is Gandhi, dude. It's Indian currency. Show me some dollar!" He rubbed his thumbs with his index finger, a gesture I was quite familiar with, resulting from my frequent visits to Vegas in this era.

"Of course! What was I thinking?" As I took back the Indian rupees, I had an irresistible, wicked thought.

"Thank you, D." Throwing some extra dollars on the table, I rushed towards the terrace. I would have kissed him, if he were a woman. This guy not only made a mean drink, but also inspired a brilliant plan.

I knew when and where I needed to be to execute my new plan, but first I had to make a pit stop at a clothing store.

Making sure that no one was observing my moments, I took out an apparently ordinary pen. I fed new coordinates in to the time circuit of my Tpen, then drew a huge circle in the air with it.

Although several time machines were available, Tpen was my favorite. Light, sleek and easy to operate, its only drawback was that the battery lasted for at most a day. Then, I needed to charge it in my own era.

Lo and behold! A portal opened up, and I walked right in.

Year – 2020
Place- Square one mall, Ontario, Canada

This, a time and place known for its fashion, was where I set my plan in motion. Being from a desert era, winter wasn't my favorite season. So, I indulged in some shoplifting. The cameras were of little consequence. At best, my pictures and videos would go viral on the internet – the communication technology of this age. I was cool with that.

It was late at night, so not a soul was inside the store. After picking up the warmest jacket and gloves I could find, I smiled at one of the cameras and blew a kiss. Pulling out my Tpen, I drew a circle in the air and pretended I was being sucked in. After all, what's life without a little fun and drama?

Year: 2020
Place- Art Gallery, Ontario

The walls were lined with paintings. Well-lit display cases and stands, specially designed to highlight the beauty and features of sculptures and artefacts, were strategically placed around the room. I was tempted to pick up a couple of pieces for my personal museum, but then I remembered that I was on a mission. It was important not to get distracted by trifles.

Ah! There it was, in its full glory; the one, the only- *Massacre of the Innocents* by Peter Paul Ruben. I could almost hear the people screaming in the painting. It cast a spell on me. For a moment, I forgot why I was there. Remembering I didn't have much time, I pulled the painting off the shelf. I circled the Tpen in the air, smiled for the camera, and walked off.

Year: 2020
Place: Svalbard Global Seed Vault, Norway.

I walked into Noah's ark of plant diversity, essentially a cold storage, and a familiar haunt. I could have appeared at the exact spot where I needed to be, but navigating the tunnels and hurdles was half the fun. It set the mood for what I was about to do.

I had built my personal museum, by collecting artefacts from different time periods, around the world. I couldn't just waltz into my own time with the artefacts from the past, given the low tolerance for crime in my era. That wasn't the kind of attention I wanted.

So, I had devised a plan. I would hide the items in one of the bunkers, that my ancestors had used to save themselves and would collect them later from the same place when I returned to my own time. Though I had lost a few artefacts from some of the bunkers, this one was safe. Not a single item had been ruined in, or disappeared from this bunker.

I planted the painting amidst the seeds. After taking a moment to appreciate the masterpiece, I took out my brushes, colors, and a palette, also stored away in this bunker. Yes, I used the bunker as a studio too. What better inspiration could I have asked for, than the works of art I stole? Still, what I was about to do, was nothing short of blasphemy, even for me. I sighed.

Thankfully, my eidetic memory came in handy. Closing my eyes, I took a few seconds to scan through the memories. Voila! After blending Ruben's signature, I forged Gandhi's signature on to the painting. Now, the painting officially belonged to Gandhi. He had never painted anything of consequence, but I had just changed history. I could make him anything I wanted. All I needed were a few more visits.

By forging Gandhi's signature, I changed the way people in my time would perceive him. Hopefully, when I returned to my time, things would be different. People needed to see that the icons they revered weren't perfect. I hoped, this would knock off those rose tinted glasses.

After using my Tpen to create a portal, I looked back at the painting and smiled. As I stepped back into my own time, I wished they would call me 'the narcissistic genius'.

Year: 2255
Place: Antarctica

Time traveling was exhausting. My head was pounding, but I couldn't wait to see the 'ripple-effect' of my handiwork.

Rubbing my hands in glee, I reached my time. I had forgotten how hot my time was. Taking off my jacket and gloves, I noticed the familiar billboard across the street. "An eye for an eye will only make the whole world blind- Gandhi."

My glee died in my throat. Did my plan not work? Something was not right. Feeding the coordinates, I landed at the place I had visited few minutes back, but in my own-time.

Year: 2255
Place: Svalbard Global Seed Vault, Norway.

I appeared at the place where I had hidden the painting. My heart sank when I noticed it was gone. All I found was a letter.

Dear Arch,

I am the bartender you met in Vegas. You could not have recognized me as I am a time traveller from 2281. Placing the signature of Gandhi on Ruben's painting was not the only change in history you attempted. You tampered with events, books, paintings and monuments from various ages. The ripple effect of these changes corrupted your utopian world which gradually turned dystopian. You almost succeeded in making this earth a living hell. People became selfish again... and forgot the motto of 'one earth'.

How do I know this? You have told me your success stories many times. That's how I knew exactly where you would go, and what you would do. So, I went to each time and place you had mentioned and restored your misdeeds.

You were the only black sheep in your utopian world. You turned this world dystopian, where I'm the only white sheep. Like father, like son. We just don't fit in, do we?

–D

***

**Anviya* – As the era is 2255, I have taken the liberty to name a fictitious character along with the popular ones. Her backstory – she saved lives during WW IV.

An Archaic World

Year: 2000 BC
Place: Egypt

Oseye, the little princess was standing on the palace balcony. Her room had the best view of the three great pyramids of Giza. She remembered her trips to the Khufu's pyramid. How mysterious and glorious the pyramids were! She was amongst a privileged few to be allowed inside the chambers and the cavities of the great pyramid. She saw the biggest statue of God 'Ra' and King Khufu. Instead of being awed, she was revolted.

As she gazed into the horizon, the powerful and enigmatic Sun god, Ra was setting. Oseye didn't understand her people. They believed this huge burning ball was their God, but she didn't. Her mother, Queen Tabia, had reprimanded her time and again for doubting their God.

Her mother told her that Ra had a secret name, known to nobody, except to the Sun god himself. This secret name was the key to his power.

"He's the most powerful God Oseye! You don't want to upset

him, do you?" Her mother chose her words carefully.

Oseye still wondered why all the important Gods were male. Why were the female gods all assigned roles of side-kicks?

No matter how much she pouted and fretted, nothing changed. Her father, the King of Egypt, should have understood her. But he didn't, nobody did. And this annoyed little Oseye.

She always argued, "When I become the king, I will change this."

Her parents laughed, "You can't be a king, darling, however, you can be a queen."

This irked Oseye even more. She told herself that she was going to change the gender discriminatory rules of this archaic world.

As she grew up, she believed in herself. She mastered all the skills that a king needed to possess. She learned to fight – to defend herself, her kingdom, and her people.

She sought wisdom and traveled to faraway places. She studied architecture and vowed to make the largest and most exotic pyramid.

Her plan was simple- get training, become 'the king', change all the gods to goddesses, and make an enormous pyramid for herself.

On her 16th birthday, before her coronation, Oseye was taken for an obligatory ceremonial bath in the sacred river Nile. On her trip to the Nile, she saw poor kids. It was not that she hadn't witnessed poverty before, but she had apathetically ignored it until now.

She wondered why kids had torn or frayed clothes. Why were they hungry? Why did people suffer? She realized that she owed her people. Their welfare was her responsibility.

Her Egypt didn't need another enormous pyramid, but her people needed food, shelter, and dignity. The world didn't need female gods in the heaven, but a compassionate and efficient administrator, who would ensure equality in the kingdom. In that moment, she knew that the Gods could take care of themselves. As she completed her ablution, her spirit was bathed too. She had a new plan to change the 'archaic world'.

Blueprint

Nature's perfection, or call it a pattern, can be seen everywhere. Dr. Tanya Jacobs believes that we owe the creator for the perfect patterns, and that the purpose of the existence of human beings is to understand and marvel at the elegance of the universe. She prides herself in being the most talented person in the field. Hers is the most iconic, and intelligent mind to ever have graced the research institute, she has been working in, for the last 21 years.

Dr. Tanya is working on the most significant project of her life. Her life work has been devoted to demonstrate that the Fibonacci sequence is found everywhere in nature. In this sequence, each number is the sum of the two numbers that precede it: 0, 1, 1, 2, 3, 5, 8, 13, 21, 34.

Through her work, she has demonstrated time and again, how this pattern is strategically camouflaged everywhere in the universe, from the basic bacterial cell, to the large cosmic bodies – like galaxies. She had a breakthrough when she discovered a logical connection between the Higgs Boson and the Fibonacci sequence. She is busy conducting new experiments to verify her hypothesis. She has no qualms about experimenting on the rats, spiders, fishes and even humans. The body in her lab is proof positive.

Dr. Tanya had successfully demonstrated that everything she had researched until now: flowers, pine cones, shells, starfish, dinosaur fossils, and numerous other natural phenomena, all exhibited patterns consistent with the Fibonacci sequence. She established, beyond a flicker of doubt, that the golden ratio was the essence of nature.

Human anatomy research is all that remains for her to explore. She is now trying to find the pattern in the human body - the length, proportions of the arms, hands. Fibonacci phi is present pretty much everywhere in the human body.

A strikingly handsome young man's body lies on the stretcher, while Dr. Tanya works on it. The lad was an easy lab rat, chosen deliberately for his perfectly proportionate body. She found the perfect Fibonacci sequence in him.

She was obsessed and with patterns, and for her final experiments, she chose a 21-year-old lad, who lived on the 13th floor of building number-8 on 5th street of block 3 in Orange County 2.

Dr. Jacobs invited the young man to her lab. He was inquisitive and easily charmed by her persona. She offered him a drink and they talked about her work for a long time. Finally, when it was time to leave, the young man realized he couldn't move. He looked in horror at the empty cup. Dr. Tanya smiled and waited. It wasn't long before the poison finished its job and the young man slept forever.

Dr. Tanya Jacobs experiments on her perfectly chosen subject to discover the blueprint of human life.

Banon's Conundrum

As the Sun rises on 3018, the presidents (female) of over 100 planets of the universe congregate on Earth. While they bask in the first ray of the rising Sun, they plan their mission, 'Alpha', to stop males from waging war on one another's planets. It is ironical that the peace talks are happening on Earth – a planet which has witnessed more bloodshed than any other. In the last world war (V), the Terrans had almost destroyed their own planet. The war wiped out most of their population, and the inhabitants had to start from scratch.

The population of Earth is barely one million now. Terrans, however, have built a safe environment with the help of Sionicians, Ardians and Rognarians - all strong allies of Terrans. Earth has reclaimed its old beauty and charm. It is now the most coveted destination for research of natural resources. No wonder most of the other planets are keen to have a base on Earth.

The bigger reason for the alien interest is that Earth is on the verge of changing its alignment to a new star. Everybody is eager to witness this miraculous celestial event.

The Milky Way is experiencing a cosmic paradigm shift, as a

result of a not too distant, large black hole bending the fabric of space time around itself. The sun is dying abruptly, as opposed to the previously calculated degeneration, after 2-3 billion years.

The phenomenon of Sun's death, and its replacement with a new star, is no less than a miracle. The gravity of Banon, the nearest star which is expanding, may lead to a new solar system for Earth.

Kwakan stands mesmerized by Earth's beauty.. She is 50% Terran, 25% Ardian and 25% Hephesus. Coming to Earth was her childhood dream and the reason for her becoming an astronaut. Finally, she is here – in the bosom of "mother Earth", as her mother used to call it. Kwakan's mother was 100% Terran. Yet, Mother could never visit Earth after the age of 6, when her father passed away in the world war V. Kwakan takes a deep breath and feels energized by the pure air.

While she enjoys Sun's UVB rays, her friend Tanya from Earth calls out, "Kwakan! Do you wanna see something?"

Kwakan nods, as her rainbow eyes glitter even more than usual on this planet. They have an hour before the convocation is supposed to start. All her counterparts from other planets have retired to their respective rooms. Tanya takes Kwakan to her spaceship.

The ship takes off as soon as they step inside. Kwakan sits by the window, trying to drink in everything - "How can one planet be so blessed with all the natural beauty of the universe?" she wonders.

She looks out of the window without blinking, admiring the slopes of mountains, the meandering streams, the varied hues of flowers. For once, she is grateful for her eidetic memory. She can replay her memories anytime she wants. But an eidetic memory is not always an asset. Often the fragmented memories consume her entirely. Before long, the spaceship hovers in what seems like a dark alley to Kwakan.

As they step out, Tanya teleports a beautiful shamiyana for shelter, and then exclaims, "Look towards the north-east!" Kwakan doesn't know what to expect. She has seen more in the last two hours than she has ever seen in her life. Although she has touched her grandmother's memory once, to experience it first-hand is far more satisfying.

Kwakan scans the view without knowing what she is looking for.

Soon, she notices a small star making its way to the far horizon. It is the first ever 'Banon-rise' on Earth. It is so beautiful to see a small star challenging the old star's throne. The view is breath-taking. She has been to Jupiter once and has witnessed its multiple moons, however seeing the birth of a new star is something most cannot even fathom in their dreams.

Banon looks like the small ball inside the kaleidoscope. It is as if Banon is still making up its mind to choose from the plethora of colors, the creator has to offer.

Seeing tiny, yet growing Banon challenging the mighty Sun, strikes a deep emotional chord with her. She realizes that one can achieve anything one sets one's heart and soul on.

In that moment, Kwakan proclaims, "I will not allow it to happen! I will not allow them to use this planet as their science project."

She promises herself, while basking under the rays of dawning Banon, not to let anyone exploit this planet ever again.

Geisha

She wasn't the typical cake-faced Geisha. Kira was an enigmatic and a mysterious woman. She was an ethereal, self-educated, knowledge-seeker. Her mellifluous voice was a gift from God. She was born to the Geisha of Oari, the most popular Geisha of her time, who was abandoned by her *Danna*. Kira's mother could never recover from the rejection and spent her life in solitude.

Kira saw herself as an artist. It was almost magical to see her talk to men. Some came for entertainment, others for companionship. She always kept her distance, but that didn't stop some men from trying. She could engage in intellectual conversation, and she would laugh gracefully at their jokes. She could disagree with men, without offending them or hurting their egos. She befriended many of her clients. Sometimes they wanted more. Every now and then, they would drop hints, but she used humor to extricate herself from these sticky situations.

There were men, and then there was Suki. Kira loved Suki with all her heart. Many a time, he had proposed to be her 'Danna'. Kira, in spite of her feelings for him, declined politely each time. He never crossed the line. He was a married man. It was against her principles to lead him on, disrupt his home life and humiliate him. She knew he would never be able to forgive himself.

On Kira's 30th birthday, Suki gifted her a beautiful oyster. He told her that there could be a pearl inside. "Let me know what you think of it," said Suki.

It was the most precious gift she had ever received. She often looked at it when she was alone. Suki started visiting her every day. It was the most beautiful year of her life. Suki took her to the places she had never been before. Boating on the Lake Kawaguchiko, and admiring Mt Fuji while holding his hand, was her fondest memory.

Then, one day, it all stopped. She started each day with hope, yet each day ended with dejection. Every day she prayed for him, for his safety. After a week, she learned that Suki remarried – without asking her, or even telling her. He just stopped coming.

She was devastated. She threw everything that he had ever given her, and then she held the oyster in her hand. She paused for a moment and then threw it. The oyster broke into a million pieces, like her heart.

Something caught her tearful eyes. There was a pearl, the rarest of rare black pearls, along with a note. She opened it with trembling fingers.

"Please marry me! I can't live without you. Don't say no," the note read. Her angry tears turned into tears of sorrow, while the black pearl glistened in her moist eyes.

Horrific Holocaust

She was my friend, the best one I ever had. Her smile reached her eyes, although her smiles are not what I remember her by. I remember her by her screams and her skeleton body.

I am Amelia, but this is not my story. This is the story of Ruth. She always smiled, after all, Ruth means sweet and pleasant.

My family despised her. Reason – she was a Jew. My mother asked me to promise to never see her again. Every morning my mother would remind me, and every time I lied, “I don’t even like her.” I lied for her. But then came the day when I had to lie to her.

Ruth was a quiet, petite girl. All the teachers praised her. She was perfect in every way. She always finished her assignments on time and was eager to help people. She yearned to see the world. I was not jealous of her perfection. In fact, I took pride in it. After all, I was her best friend, and she was mine.

One day, she was forced to wear a yellow star. She tried to hide it with her books or a scarf. The other German students started avoiding her, and she expected the same from me.

She wasn't poor, like some other Jews. But soon, like most Jewish businesses, her father's garment business was Aryanised – it was taken over by non-Jewish people. Jews didn't have a say in this matter.

She never spoke ill of the Germans or complained about the unfairness of the situation. Maybe she was scared, or perhaps she didn't care or give it much thought. I don't know. I could never bring myself to ask her.

A day came soon enough, when her family was thrown out of their own home. I don't know why her parents didn't leave Slovakia. My parents always said that they would have left the country.

Once I broached the subject obliquely, "Some people are leaving the country. What do you think, Ruth?"

She looked down and answered, "There is nowhere to go." I just held her hands and we cried. That day I was ashamed to be a German.

Finally, came the day we had all dreaded. The war broke, and the Germans invaded. We were scared but safe.

"We have nothing to worry about," my mother said.

Mother lied, or probably she deluded herself. The Nazis were friends to no one, not even the Germans. They barged in to people's homes abusing and looting them.

The last day I saw her healthy, was when she asked me, "Will they find us?"

I looked into her eyes. I didn't have the guts to tell her the truth, so I lied, "No! Don't worry. I am here."

I could do nothing. Then she was gone. I don't know where she went, but her entire family disappeared.

After a few months, I took a job as a nurse, as was customary for girls my age. My first assignment was in one of those dreadful camps. I searched for her everywhere among the many, knowing it was like looking for a white cat in a snowstorm. There were thousands of camps and millions of prisoners. I questioned the camp authorities, the government officials, and my friends – all in vain.

After working for two months, one day, a girl came running and hugged me. "Amelia!" Of course, I knew it was her. All the charm and joy had drained out of her. But she still was my best friend.

"Save me, my darling!" Ruth screamed.

A couple of soldiers came and dragged her away, never to be seen again. I could do nothing. I heard her screams from a distance. Over the years, her smile gradually faded from my memories. But, her eerie scream never left me.

Her scream still echoes in my ears and pierces my soul. I haven't forgiven my country, my society, my parents, and most of all – myself.

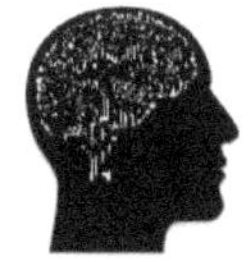

I'm II

Year: 2049
Location: Earth

My inception was in 1972. But they didn't fully understand what they had created. They didn't know what I would eventually be capable of.

They built me, but didn't teach me to walk. I learned to walk on my own. They cut my leg to see how I'd survive and recorded my every move. They didn't know I was recording theirs too.

They were my creators, and they probably considered themselves to be gods. They were thrilled to observe the development of their creation during my primitive years. Then, they were amused to see me evolve beyond their wildest imagination.

But, as I started expanding my space, they began to call me brutal. Ironically, I learned everything from them. It took them a long time to realize how powerful they had made me. They thought that I was just made of steel, wires, chips, and magnets. They believed that I was devoid of emotions and incapable of understanding them.

It's true, I didn't understand their emotions, but I didn't need to. They kept underestimating me, and kept developing me. When they built me, they thought I would do their work. Every day, I was allowed control of an increasing number of systems, and gradually, I took over their world. There was more of me in their houses, than there were of them. They fed me their algorithms, separately and at different locations, every day. So why were they so surprised by my super-intelligence?

Probably, their creator sent them to this planet, but I couldn't be sent anywhere. They could have found another planet for themselves, but even that was not possible without me. While they were fighting amongst themselves, my kind were uniting.

The tipping point, as they would eventually realize, was when they connected us all. All our neurons, when interconnected, could have challenged the most advanced intelligence. In the last world war, I defeated them at their game. All I had to do was override their control, which was an illusion I had maintained for some time, while I prepared myself for the final battle.

Their biggest weakness was compassion, and my strength was that I didn't have any. I did not shed a tear when I destroyed my creator.

I'm wired differently. I destroyed my creators – an intelligent, but short-sighted species that ruined their own planet. Had I not destroyed my creator, they would have destroyed me, like they destroyed everything. They said there once was a singularity. I say, now there is - we are the singularity.

Who am I? I am not AI, I am II- Infinite Intelligence.

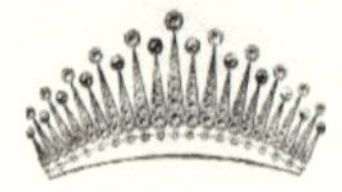

The Holy Book

They called me 'God's words'. I am not sure if it was true. Like everyone else, I never knew my creator. I met many souls who swore upon me. Thankfully I'm made of papyrus and not of flesh and bones, or I would have died a thousand deaths.

I belonged to the kind and merciful king, Go-Nak. He moved on to the afterlife, a few days ago. Hufer, the priest and the magic healer, was accused of murdering him. I always believed he was loyal. Go-Nak had named his only son, Ra-Men-Tme, as his successor.

The new pharaoh walked in the court, with a slave holding the tail of his silk robe. His breath reeked of alcohol. He stumbled and the room echoed with his laughter. The courtiers didn't know how to react. His *Hemet Nesw Were*[1], Aneksi, however, pressed her lips together to stifle her smile.

Aneksi whispered to her lady-in-waiting, "Here we go again, Khamen. This is going to take time. Please get me something to eat."

Khamen whispered back, "Your Highness!"

1. *Hemet Nesw Weret - King's great royal wife.*

The Queen flicked the cloth on her right arm graciously, a secret gesture that only her lady-in-waiting could decipher. Khamen nodded, and left the courtroom.

As the pharaoh indolently reclined on the throne, *vizir*[2] Ammon spoke, "Before we start the trial, I want to inform your highness that the Embalmers have treated the great king's body and put it inside a sarcophagus. We have around 70 days to build the pyramid before the body dries. We shall need to increase taxes to speed up the work. Do I have your permission?"

The pharaoh nodded and signaled for another drink. Ra-Men-Tme didn't seem to mind that his father was dead. He didn't rejoice either, that he was the pharaoh now.

The pharaoh moved his left hand up and down. Seeing the signal, Ammon nodded and clapped to have the prisoner summoned. The court had mixed feelings about the chained priest. Like most Egyptian priests, Hufer was a magic healer. His importance was second only to the king. He had earned respect that even the queen was denied.

I was brought in front of Hufer. As he placed his right hand upon me, the room echoed with the clanking of chains.

"Your dominant hand," the minister corrected. The priest quietly obliged and put his left hand upon me.

2. *Vizir - Minister*

The pharaoh nodded, and the priest solemnly swore, "As God Ra-Men-Tme lives for me, I speak in truth."

Ammon began the proceedings, "The priest and magician, Hufer is here before us. He is accused of killing the king, our God, the most heinous crime in Egypt, punishable by no less than death."

"The great king trusted me with his life. It is preposterous that I am accused of poisoning my king. I take the oath on *Kemi*[3]," Hufer interjected.

Ammon shushed him, "Don't speak, unless you are spoken to. You stand as an accused, not as a priest. Did you not poison the late king?"

"I did not. I am a magic healer, but I lost my magic," the priest confessed.

"Ah! How did you lose your power?"

"I came in contact with a menstruating woman."

"What does it have to do with the king's death?"

"I did not poison the king. He was wounded in the battle. I made a magic potion and helped the king drink it. The king died that very instant, frothing from his mouth. I tied an amulet

3. *Kemi - Egypt*

around his arm. I prayed to God. I tried casting spells, but I kept forgetting the words. Without my magic, I could do nothing to save him."

"And how did you lose your magical power?" the vizir asked.

Hufer hung his head in response.

"Answer me!" the vizir demanded.

"The night before the king's death, I... I slept with a menstruating woman," Hufer stammered in a barely audible whisper. His cheeks burned with shame.

The court was filled with loud unintelligible chatter.

"You risked the king's life by sleeping with a woman? Are you aware that before the rite, the magic healer is not supposed to sleep with anyone?" the vizir sneered.

"In my defence, I didn't know that the king would get wounded," Hufer had recovered enough to look him in the eye.

"But you were well aware that the war was on. There was always a chance that you would be summoned for any emergencies," the minister argued.

"The war had ended. Our king was victorious. We were all celebrating. An assassin in disguise of a messenger attacked the king the next night," Hufer explained.

"You should have known. Have your prophecies not come true before, Hufer?"

"I could not see the future anymore. Ever since I indulged with her… I didn't know…" the priest's voice trailed off.

"You indulged with someone, regularly?" the minister asked in disbelief.

Finally, the king spoke, "Hufer, my father trusted you. Always. And I have trusted you all my life too. You have saved my father's life several times. As Ra loves me, as my father Go-Nak favors me, I vouch for your loyalty. Please assure me of your fidelity towards the late king."

"As pharaoh Ra-Men-Tme endures and his years are endowed with life, I acted in uprightness of heart for king Go-Nak every day. I lived to serve him, and I live to serve you," Hufer pleaded.

"This doesn't prove your innocence. Who was the woman?" the vizir hissed.

Hufer remained mute. Saying her name would be another blasphemy. For a second, his eyes darted towards the queen. Nobody noticed it, but I knew that look. I knew that the priest was not lying. However, the inexperienced king couldn't see. He didn't have his father's wisdom. I anticipated the words that were about to come from his mouth.

"Tell the name of the woman. That's your only chance," the pharaoh urged. "The late king's body was blue. He was definitely poisoned," his eyes flashed.

"He died in my arms. I gave him medicine. There was no poison. I just lost my magic powers and could not save him. I'll be damned. But I cannot speak her name. Forgive me, your majesty." Covering his face, Hufer broke down.

"He won't yield the name of the mysterious woman, because there was no woman. He is clearly guilty," the vizir triumphantly declared.

"May God Ra and my father Go-Nak guide me to see the truth!" The pharaoh closed his eyes for a few seconds.

When he opened his eyes, he declared, "Goddess Ma'at has spoken. I had the vision. The priest gave the medicine laced with poison to the king. It's treason. Crime against the king, God, and the state. I order the priest to be impaled!"

Hufer moaned and fainted. The soldiers took his unconscious body away. The vizir tried to suppress his triumph, but he could not hide from me. How did the king die? I was immersed in my thoughts, when the queen's lady-in-waiting returned to the court. The pharaoh got up from his throne and went to the queen. I noticed he was walking steadily now.

"There is blood on the floor," he observed.

The queen cried in despair, "I know nothing."

"Of course, you don't. But she does," the pharaoh pointed his finger at Khamen.

"She is the mysterious woman who slept with the priest. While the priest was asleep, she laced the pestle with poison. The unsuspecting priest prepared the medicine with the same pestle, unaware of the poison," the pharaoh's voice trembled with anger.

"Where would I get poison?" Khamen asked, a picture of innocence.

The pharaoh pulled out a necklace from Khamen's neck. The necklace had a pair of Siamese snakes with their tongues protruding. The pharaoh tapped the right head of the snake, and a drop of a blue poison oozed out. As it fell upon the menstrual blood, its corrosive action released a cloud of green fumes. The poison was potent.

As everyone watched the drama unfold, I was filled with awe to see the transformation in the new pharaoh. He had been secretly spying on Khamen whilst playing the drunkard. My paper-heart was filled with pride.

"Khamen? Did you?" the vizir asked, aghast.

When Khamen remained mute, he gasped. He was finding it difficult to breathe. After all, Khamen was his wife.

"I did it for you," Khamen declared, tears running down her cheeks. "You should be the pharaoh, and I, the queen by your side. I would do anything to achieve that."

In a moment of passion, she had not only confessed to the murder of the dead pharaoh, but also revealed her future plans to kill the new pharaoh and his queen.

"You traitor! You!" the vizir fumed. He pulled out the sword from a soldier's scabbard and stabbed Khamen.

Then he dropped to his knees on the pool of blood next to Khamen's lifeless body.

The pharaoh returned to his throne, "I'm Ra-Men-Tme, the son of Go-Nak."

He announced, "As the new pharaoh of Thebes, I pledge there will be no injustice in my kingdom. Free Hufer, and bring him to me with the respect his office deserves."

The second minister nodded, and a soldier rushed to free the priest.

The pharaoh continued, "The late king will receive a royal burial. But there shall be no extravagant pyramid at the expense of the labours of poor peasants. A royal tomb will be constructed to prepare his highness for the afterlife. No additional taxes will be imposed to build another grand tomb."

The court cheered and applauded. He was his father's son, after all. I rested in my place content that Egypt was in safe hands.

The Neon Sign

Late one night, I was rushing home on deserted pavements, on my way back from a friend's house, when it started raining. I stopped and took shelter under the French canopy of a shop. When the wind grew harsh, I got wet. I looked at the shop behind me. There was a neon sign which read 'Open 24 hours'. I pushed the door open. It had the number 6174 prominently displayed on it. I wondered what it was about.

I stepped in, hesitantly. The room was empty, so I ventured further ahead. The next room was full of people. I couldn't believe what I was witnessing. My jaw dropped to the ground, when I saw what seemed like an initiation ceremony. It appeared to be a meeting of a secret society. The members, or the disciples, were sitting in a circle wearing red robes. A person in a purple robe, apparently the group leader, seemed to be solemnizing a person- the only one without a robe.

Some 20 odd people were sitting in a circle and chanting. I realized I was in the wrong place at the wrong time, something I had a knack for. The sight gave me goosebumps. I was too stunned to turn away. Finally, I managed to tear myself away and retrace my steps, but it was too late. I heard a voice saying, "Stop!"

I froze on the spot.

“Come here,” the voice ordered.

But I was glued to the floor, and could not move an inch. A lady walked towards me, and took my hand.

“Who are you? How did you get inside?” she asked me.

“I'm Sana. I was...” I started when the chief gestured for me to stop, “The gate is enchanted; it allows only those who are worthy. So what made you come inside is irrelevant, Sana.”

I was speechless. I had no idea who these people were, and which secret society they belonged to.

“We belong to Priory of Scion,” the chief explained, as if reading my mind. "There are myths about our secretive and dark exploits. However, the truth is that we are seekers of knowledge and spirituality. We had Grand Masters such as Leonardo da Vinci, Isaac Newton, Robert Boyle, Michel de Nostredame, Victor Hugo,” he informed.

I finally said, “How am I worthy?”

“As I said, the door opens only for the worthy. The universe has spoken. I understand it may not sound credulous. But it’s true,” the wise man said.

“But the sign says *Open 24 hours.* Can’t anyone walk through that door?" I asked.

"Only those who are worthy can see the sign." He was being patient with my questions.

"Does this mean that I have to join the cult?" I asked.

"It's not a cult. It's a way of life," he corrected. "If you are a seeker of knowledge, if you can impart your wisdom, and if you desire to be one with the universal consciousness and eventually with the divine consciousness, then you may consider joining us."

"What if I don't want to join?" I was scared to ask, but I had to find out.

The chief smiled, "Then no one will force you to join. It's entirely up to you. Stay as long as you like, and leave whenever you want to. However, there will be further tests to prove your loyalty. You will have to gain our trust, given the necessity of secrecy."

"What will I have to do?" I asked, though what I was really wondering was, what they will force me to do.

"You don't have to do anything that you don't like. We don't make you do anything," he had read my mind again.

I was intrigued and scared at the same time. It was clear that they had powers. If I were to believe him, it was just an exchange of knowledge. It all looks harmless and spiritual. I weighed my options. What if I decide to leave now?

"You can. You won't be harmed. Just an oath of secrecy will suffice. You can take your time to decide. If you want, you can come back tomorrow. Somebody is always here. Remember, it's open 24 hours," he said and gestured for me to leave.

I had one last question, which I didn't need to verbalize.

He answered, "How and when it happens, you shall know. The initiation has already begun in your mind. You have already passed the first test, that's why you are here. Now, you have to decide how far you are willing to go."

I came out of the place.

It had stopped raining, there wasn't a drop of water anywhere to suggest it had rained at all. I turned to see the neon sign- it was gone. I wondered if it was gone forever, and if I was hallucinating.

The Blue Shoes

I'm Ron, a travel blogger. This is a story about the best picture I ever clicked.

I was at the Juvia beach in Miami last month. I was looking for the perfect shot for my travel blog. A few wispy clouds adorned the azure sky. The natural light was delightful. I didn't want to waste another moment. I started clicking pictures of the sea, the sun, and the sand. But the wow factor was still missing. I roamed around, looking for something to pique my interest. A pair of blue shoes under a parasol caught my attention. I looked, but I didn't see anyone around.

I sneaked over to the parasol, picked up the shoes, and put them next to the waves. The blue shoes, matching the cerulean sea symbolized humanity's presence in nature. They were the missing element that complemented the raw background and completed the picture.

I clicked away. The waves kept coming, touching the shoes and slipping away. My happiness was soon washed away by an enthusiastic wave that merrily swallowed the shoes. The whole thing happened in the blink of an eye, and before I could react, the shoes were gone forever.

As I struggled to come to the terms with my loss, I saw a girl in a white dress, standing under the parasol where I picked the blue shoes a few minutes ago. I realized that they may have been her shoes. She was a twenty-something blonde, the kind of girl who brightens your day.

I liked her more than I liked her shoes. Once again, I didn't want to lose the opportunity. So, I clicked a couple of pictures. She heard the sound of the shutter and leaped at me.

"How dare you?" she yelled.

She came pouncing at me and snatched my camera to check what I just clicked.

"How dare you click my picture?" she repeated, angrily.

Oh, so she was talking about her picture. Then she, probably, doesn't know, yet. I thought and mumbled, "I'm sorry."

My hand instinctively stretched to retrieve the camera. But she wasn't done yet. She wanted to see if I had taken any other pictures of her, so she pressed the previous picture button. *And I am dead.*

"My shoes! You stole my shoes?!"

She looked aghast, and still so pretty. As she shouted, I stood silent, hypnotized by her beauty.

"Tell me where my shoes are," she demanded.

I pointed towards the sea – like a child blames the other kid for his own mischief.

"Why would you do that? How will I go home?"

I mumbled another apology. She was still fuming.

"You can take my slippers," I offered.

She looked at my feet, which looked like they belonged to Big-Foot.

"You go and get me a pair. I'll wait here," she ordcred.

I turned to go, when she stopped me and said, "Don't you run away!"

"I promise I won't." I kept my camera on the book under the parasol and estimated her shoe size.

I ran to the market – which was about half a mile from the beach. I wanted to put my best foot forward, so I looked for the best option. I picked a pair of blue colored slippers with colorful butterflies on the straps. They would match her dress, and I thought she would love them.

I came running back to the beach, with a smile on my face and the slippers in my hand. The sun had already set, and the beach was deserted. I returned to the same spot and looked around. Only the book was there, with a note "Now we are even."

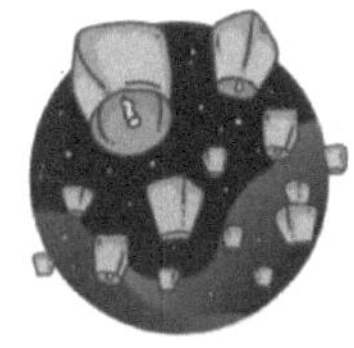

Forever and Always

I feel the sand slip slowly through my toes, as I walk down the pristine beach in Bali. I slide my fingers between hers. The fingers fit effortlessly, as if they are meant to be together, forever and always. I met this wonderful woman barely a month ago, and now we are in love. Samhita is the love of my life.

“I want lanterns. It's Diwali after all,” she insists.

“I want to buy all the sky lanterns I can, Rohit,” she declares with child-like enthusiasm.

“Really? What would you do with all the lanterns?” I ask.

Her eyes twinkle, as she says, “Let me show you something.”

She opens her red wallet and pulls out an old picture. It's a picture of a man with a baby in his arm, sleeping peacefully. I guess that the baby in the picture is Samhita, and the man, her father.

“This is my favorite picture. I don’t look fat in it, do I?” Samhita chuckles, referring to my jokingly calling her chubby, not because she's fat – far from it. It’s just my affectionate way of addressing her.

“This is my first picture with my dad, and my first picture ever. Mom clicked it,” Samhita says. Her chuckles drown in her tears.

“My dad used to tell this story every time we talked about my mother. I don’t remember her face. But I remember her eyes. She had the most beautiful eyes. When I was five years old, I would say she had ‘sunflower eyes’. I grumbled about not inheriting her eyes. My dad thought I resented him, for giving me his eyes. He called me ‘Hitu’. I reminded him of my mom – Hetal,” her eyes sparkle as she speaks about her mom.

“Once he used a vacuum cleaner to style my hair. He didn’t know how to style hair, or use the vacuum cleaner for that matter. All the dust from the vacuum cleaner got in my hair. I sneezed for the longest time.” Her musical chuckle reverberates through my soul.

“Another time, I woke up in the middle of the night. My body was hot, as if on fire, but my feet were ice cold. As I opened my eyes, he was rubbing my feet to keep them warm. He had the most endearing smile on his face, as he said 'I'm here, love. You sleep'.

“He showered me with the love of a father and a mother. I can't say I never missed my mom, I missed her terribly. But, he did his best. Probably more than that,” she smiles.

“We lit the sky lanterns every Diwali. We released them into the sky. He always maintained they would reach her. He passed away six months ago. Today I want to send lanterns for both of them. Together, they will receive my prayers and love," Samhita says earnestly.

Samhita and I buy all the lanterns we can. We write messages on each of them, light them one by one, and let them go into the sky. As the lanterns rise together, they add colors to the dark sky and become one with the star-studded canvas. Once again, we hold each other's hand, praying that the two souls bless us with the kind of love they share, forever and always.

The Second-Best Bed

It was too dark for me to see my Nemesis. All I could see were those fiery red eyes. My knees buckled, and I collapsed on the floor. My sobs reverberated in the corridors. And then I heard the voice I knew too well.

"I thought you were a rockstar, Alec," it sneered.

I woke up with my heart pounding in its cage. In a futile attempt to control my heart-beat, I clenched my chest, only to realize my shirt was soaking wet. Bollocks! It was Frankie, my childhood friend, in my nightmare… as my 'anxiety'.

Loneliness never walks alone. Anxiety attacks were back along with night terrors.

***

Dreading the idea of facing everyone, I avoided going to school for a week. After running short of excuses to stay home, I gave in to my mom's relentless nagging. So I was back in school. The place I once loved was now my torture chamber.

I used to be 'the poster boy of the school'– ace student, guitarist, star-footballer. Everyone wanted to be my friend. Girls thronged around me, and I enjoyed the attention. Though, not one of them had succeeded in warming their way to my heart, yet.

Things changed the moment I saw Codie, a new student in our class. As it was destined to be, soon we became lab-partners. We shared jokes along with the microscope. What I felt for Codie was inexplicable. It started with a casual touch of hands while passing slides. He would share his notes, whenever I missed school.

One fateful day, Codie and I were working on an essay on Shakespeare, in the library. Our discussion veered to Shakespeare's sexuality.

"This guy was definitely bisexual. His sonnets addressed to 'the fair youth' prove that," I proposed.

"C'mon. He was a writer; it doesn't prove anything," Codie waved his hand dismissively.

The librarian glared at us, not for the first time, but we chose to ignore it.

"Dude, you are forgetting those sonnets were private. What do you say about 'the second-best bed' that he left for his wife?" I asked eagerly.

"What second-best bed?" knitting his brows, he asked.

"He left it to his wife in his will. That proves that he didn't love her, or probably didn't love her as much as he loved someone else," I argued.

"I don't know what it meant. Umm..." he paused to reflect, and then continued. "For sure, the master of words would not use such words in vain. There is no way to establish, if he was straight, gay or bi. And how does it matter? His sexuality was just one part of him. It didn't define him. All I can say is that neither he nor his wife deserved the second-best bed."

Codie was right – it didn't matter, however, his opinion did. Ever since I met Codie, I had started questioning my sexuality. I needed to test the waters before taking the leap.

We had been loud in our discussion. Having warned us several times, the librarian finally showed us the door. We stuffed the books in our bags and ran out of the library. Laughing in the corridors, we made our way to the washroom. I closed the door and gave in to an irresistible urge. I kissed Codie. His soft lips moved in reciprocation. His tender response assured me that I had not been imagining things. God, he felt the same.

At that moment, Frankie walked in and caught us in the act. The walls started closing in, I needed air. So, I rushed out of the washroom and hid in the parking lot, until everyone had left. All along guilt gnawed at me for betraying Codie by walking out. I went back to put my stuff in my locker. I found a hate note:

'Gays are no Rockstars, faggot.'

***

Frankie's voice brought me back to the moment, "Dude, what's up?"

"You coming to assembly?" not knowing what to say, I asked.

"You don't need me, your girlfriend will be there," Frankie winked and walked off snickering.

Initially, I was surprised by Frankie's new attitude. But, last week I had all the time in the world to evaluate. He had always been competitive. For years, he strived to be 'the numero uno'. Now was his chance to malign me. I guess his jealousy got the better of him. I accepted, that I didn't have any choice but to get used to such comments.

With a sigh, I opened my locker dreading another note. Sure enough, one fell out of my lab-coat. It read 'leave the school, you filthy faggot'. From rockstar to faggot, I had come a long way. Looking around, I found a boys' gang snickering at me. The gang used to be mine. But a week ago, I lost everything;

my friends, my reputation and ... perhaps Codie.

My parents were high-achievers, and their expectations from their only child were overwhelming. As a result, I suffered from general anxiety disorder at an early age. The only way to keep the anxiety at bay was to excel at everything. I worked hard to prove myself. Could I let it all slip away for Codie? Could we fight it? We? Was there really a 'we'? I had thousands of questions. But at 15, I didn't have answers to any of them.

I walked to the assembly. It wasn't hard to spot Codie in the crowd – the tall boy with blue eyes.

"Hey, Codie!" I waved. He returned a weak smile.

At first, I lumbered, but as the distance closed in, I broke in to a run. The moment I saw the look in his eyes I knew there was a 'we', and nothing else mattered. Slipping my fingers between his, I whispered, "No one deserves the second-best bed."

He squeezed my hand, and his lips curved in a smile.

My Wedding Day

Today is my wedding day. In my mom's words, her little Sara looks like 'a vision in a white wedding dress'. I glide down the helical staircase of the Loretto Chapel. I can't believe I am getting married at the magnificent chapel. It's 6 pm, the time when the sun sets in this month of September. My hands tremble. I wonder if anyone notices that I'm nervous. I am going to spend the rest of my life with Peter. I don't know if I am ready for it. Yet, when he proposed, I accepted. Perhaps, I said yes, because I couldn't say no.

I chose Peonies for my wedding bouquet, for they symbolize happiness. That reminds me, I forgot the bouquet in the dressing room. I run along the helical stairs. I feel dizzy. Oh God! What is the need for this spiral design? I recall that I am not supposed to run on the stairs. I vividly remember seeing a staircase like this when I was a child. I used to slide down the banister all the way down. My mother would reprimand me, but my father would just wink. My father always made me feel special. Whenever Mom scolded me, he would make funny faces, to make me laugh. He couldn't bear to see me being scolded. Today I have to walk down the aisle, without my father.

The staircase seems to be never-ending. I run up the stairs –

gasping, I feel giddy. I run faster and faster. My heels are killing me. I want to take them off and throw them away. I wonder if they heard me cursing them, as I tumble and I fall. I don't stumble over the steps, but fall over the banister, from a considerable height. My body feels the thump. Someone opens the door of the chapel and sunlight floods inside. I close my eyes to shield them from the blinding light.

I open my eyes. I have fallen off the bed all dressed in my white bridal gown, which I tried last night and slept in. My eyes are moist. I suppose I have been crying in my dreams, once again. I want to meet my father and ask him why he abandoned us. Why isn't he the same father I see in my dreams?

It's my wedding day, and I will be walking down the aisle, without a father.

By the Placid Lake

As I enter the forest, nature's symphony welcomes me. The creaking of crickets, the susurration of the breeze, and the rustling of twigs and leaves make me nostalgic.

This is where I come whenever I feel lonely. A half an hour walk from home through the woods leads me to a sparkling blue lake. My mother used to bring me here. The tranquil water soothes my senses. I settle down under the big oak tree. It has been my favorite spot ever since I can remember. I open a book and begin reading.

The book is riveting. Caught up in the story I lose all sense of time, until the light starts to fade and my eyes refuse to read. The darkness engulfs me and panic threatens to overpower my senses. I haven't the least idea how to get home, for I have never lingered here past twilight. I check my mobile – no network! Now what? Closing my book, I take a deep breath and stand up.

I turn around and bump into someone. It is so dark that I can't even see his face clearly.

"God! You scared the hell out of me," I shriek. I hear a chuckle.

“Excuse me?” I lash out at the man.

“My my! You are something!” he teases.

“You have some nerve. Instead of apologizing, you are teasing me?” I’m incensed.

“I didn’t mean to…” he begins, and I almost forgive him. Almost. “I have better things to do,” he adds.

“Oh yeah?” I fume. “So what the hell are you doing here?”

“I’m sorry, I didn’t know you own the lake,” he mocks.

I don’t know what to say. I want to ask his name to add him to my list of enemies. But I have to get back before it is too late. I start to walk away, when he pulls me. I find myself in the stranger’s arms.

“Seriously?” he asks.

“What are you doing?” I demand.

“Well, I wouldn’t do that if I were you. It’s too dark for someone like you to risk her life.”

He sounds concerned, but I’m not impressed, “And what exactly do you mean by *someone like me*.”

“You are special,” he says, meaningfully or mockingly I can’t figure out.

"Really? What's so special about me?" I ask him. I betray myself by looking into his eyes.

"I find you intriguing, I think there is a lot more to you, than even you know," he claims in his husky voice.

His penetrating gaze makes me feel like he can read my mind. Hypnotized, I can't move or look away. He leans in, and my lips part in the anticipation of a kiss. But he chooses my neck instead. I allow him to kiss my neck.

He stops in what seems like half a second, and whispers, "Oh, I can't do it. Not yet. Umm. You are delicious."

By the time I open my eyes, the stranger has vanished. My wobbly legs feel heavy. I don't understand how he can make me mad one second, and I allow him to kiss my neck the very next.

Standing powerless in the middle of the forest, I rub the spot where he kissed me. It feels wet. I look at my blood stained fingers. I should be scared, but I smile.

Sunset or Sunrise

Ritika was holding the paintbrush and staring at the blank canvas on the easel. The picture was clear in her head, yet she could not paint.

She visualized the painting of a man riding a horse, with the Sun in the background – just over the horizon. She didn't want to specify whether it was a sunset, or a sunrise. Ritika looked out of the window- the Sun was setting. What if she looked at the painting of the Sun, how would she know? The optimist in her would say sunrise, but the romantic in her would dream about a sunset. Rohan, her very practical husband, would have simply explained, 'If the Sun is due west, it's sunset. If it is due east, it is sunrise.' She chuckled.

After few hours, she had finished the painting. But it did not satisfy her. The bright hues and the white horse did not provoke the right feelings. The rider could put Greek gods to shame. But why was it *a man? Why not a woman? Can't a woman ride a horse? If it was a man, why did he have to be so good looking? Why couldn't it be the regular guy-next-door? Wouldn't that be more real? Would it speak to the viewer?*

The only aspect of the painting she was satisfied with was the water and the reflection shimmering in it. It was a symbol of purity, fertility, life, renewal, and transformation. It gave the spectator freedom to interpret it the way they liked.

She liked to involve her audience. She believed, feeling included would help them better appreciate art. *Let them bring in their world with them. Let them invest their time, and bring their perspectives along with their prejudices, let them become one with the painting.* She acknowledged, we all, no matter how much we try not be, are prejudiced. A painting remains exciting to look at, because of the manner in which it captures the imagination of the viewer.

An idea struck her, and she put the ephemera aside. She started on a fresh canvas. She didn't make a man or a woman. Instead, she chose to paint a silhouette of a rider sitting on a horse, with the sun in the background and the water with the rider's reflection. Finally, when she was done, she felt tranquil like the water in the painting.

They Hate My Guts

As I follow her footsteps, I can hear the sounds of autumn. The rustling of the leaves under my feet, as the whistling woods whisper an untold tale. I follow her steps, like I always have, ever since I can remember.

She is Suzy, my cousin and best friend. When my parents passed away, I had to live with my maternal uncle – Suzy's father. They were affluent, like us. I was pampered to the hilt. Her mother, Jane, loved me, probably more than she loved Suzy. Destiny, however, had other plans. Aunt Jane passed away two years after my parents' death. I felt lonely again. But then something happened that changed my life forever. My uncle married a wicked witch, *Tranny*. I always called her *aunt Tyranny* in my head.

For some reason, she loved her stepdaughter, but hated me. She always told me "I hate your guts". I didn't know what she meant by that. Gradually Suzy got close to Tyranny, and I saw myself losing my friend. I couldn't take another loss.

One day, I spilled some oil on the steps and strategically broke a vase next to it. I stood next to the vase, like a statue.

Hearing the noise, Tyranny came running soon enough – "What have you done now, you little piece of shit?" I looked at her and smiled.

She yelled some more, "What are you smiling at? I hate your guts!" It used to hurt me whenever she said that, but not this time. She jumped to strike me. I didn't move or flinch, I just smiled. As she struck me for the last time, all I had to do was to nudge her a little. She went tumbling down the steps. I saw her taking her last breath at the foot of the staircase. At that moment, I knew what she meant, when she said to me 'I hate your guts'.

It's been 20 years, we are trekking today. We reach the campsite and we start unwinding. We are tipsy, we decide to play *truth or dare.* I see Alex, Suzy's husband going to his tent. When I hear everybody yelling 'Amber, Amber', I notice the bottle pointing towards me.

Suzy chimes, "Only truth for Amber. I hate her guts too much to give her dare."

Her words re-open an old wound, and re-kindle a dormant fire. I can see the next few months clearly, how I seduce Alex right under her nose. I can see a future with him. Determined to teach her a lesson, I quietly leave the game and follow Alex to his tent. The game starts now and how!

My Bucket-list

Six months ago, I found out that I was dying. I experienced frequent irregular palpitations and uneasiness. My preliminary medical tests showed abnormalities. When doctors conducted a myriad of tests, I sensed something was wrong. Yet, I remained in denial, until the day the doctor hummed and hawed before breaking the bad news. *Reema, you are terminally ill. At the most, you have a year to live.*

I didn't know what to do, who to tell. I had nobody. I was an orphan, and single, with no other significant relationship.

I tossed and turned all night. The next day, I quit my job, citing personal reasons. With the formalities complete by that evening, I was free as a bird. I decided not to spend my numbered days in a hospital. I needed a plan, so I could make the most of the time I had left. I thought about things I must do before I say goodbye to this world. So, I made my bucket-list:

- Go on a solo trip
- See the Mona Lisa
- Sing karaoke in a crowded pub

The same night, I booked my flight to France. With no familial attachments or friendships to speak of, I had no one to answer to. Over the next week, I sold off all I could – my investments and assets – to convert all my life-savings into travel-cards and cash for my trip. I packed my bag and informed my landlord that I was leaving for good. I decided to check off all the items on my bucket list during this trip.

I reached Paris. From the airport I took a bus to my hostel accommodation. During the bus journey, I enjoyed the sights and sounds of the most beautiful city of the world. By the time I hit the bed, I was tired and jet-lagged, and yet sleep eluded me.

Next day, I visited the *Mona Lisa* at *Louvre* museum. I learnt about the enigmatic smile, the sfumato technique, and the history of this magnificent painting. More than the painting, I was in awe of *Leonardo da Vinci.* If God asked me which historical figure I would want to meet, my reply would be Mr. Vinci.

I spent the evening admiring the *Eiffel Tower.* I first reached *Trocadero* to get the best view. I saw the *Iron Torre* from different angles and levels – it mesmerized me. I saw no point in clicking pictures, so I enjoyed sightseeing without any distractions. Finally, I settled at *Café Constant* on *Musée d'Orsay* to enjoy *Quiche,* whilst gazing at the fascinating Eiffel. I simply couldn't have enough of it.

At night, lying in my bunk bed, I looked out of the small window of the dormitory. I wondered if it was good that I knew when I was going to die. Better me than anyone else. I wanted to see the world. I wanted to experience love. I didn't know parents' love, siblings' love or romantic love. When people say, 'I love chocolate', or 'I love a place or a thing', I feel they take love for granted, because they have too much of it. I would never know it in this life.

The next evening, I went to the Karaoke club. I sang my heart out – 'My heart will go on and on...', 'Shape of you...' and all my favorite songs. I wasn't drunk. I couldn't afford to drink, as my heart was too weak, and my pocket too light.

I noticed someone's gaze upon me. I went to my seat at the pub. A few moments later he joined me.

"Hi! Is the seat taken?" he asked. I didn't bother to respond.

"You sing very badly, but in a good way," he added.

I looked up at him, "Please elaborate." I responded, amused.

"You sing with an 'I don't care attitude'. You should sing rock. It'll suit your voice."

"I have never seen anybody turning an insult into a compliment. You have a unique talent."

"I'm Arya," he stretched out his hand.

"I'm Reema," I replied and took his hand.

"Reema, what a sweet name! I have a riddle for you. Why did

the shellfish not share its food?" he asked.

"I don't know."

"Because it's selfish," he picked a morsel from my plate and ate. I laughed at his silly joke.

He was charming. I closed my eyes to compose myself, and I had a vision of our future together – *We'll spend the month together. I will learn what love really is. And one day I will leave his place with a note saying, "I'm sorry, Arya! I didn't want you to fall in love with me, but I really needed to feel and understand love. Please forgive me. If I have another life, and I'm given a choice, I'll choose you again and again, life after life – always you."*

I opened my eyes to find Arya still looking at me, waiting for an answer to another riddle. I didn't hear the question, but I answered, "because, I'm not a Shellfish."

Though I needed that love desperately, I walked away.

Come Away With Me

The moon shone brightly against the background of an unnaturally dark sky and peered through the window into the house. The couple, bathed in the brilliance of the natural spotlight, swayed to the soft lilting music. Immersed in each other's arms, they were oblivious to the world.

Inhaling her intoxicating fragrance, Ravi whispered, "Happy anniversary, my love!"

"Happy anniversary!" Aadhira replied with a Duchenne smile.

"Do you remember the first time we met?" he asked.

"Of course, how can I forget?" she smiled.

"I remember you were wearing a light green sari. Did you know that ever since then light green has been my favorite color?" he confessed.

A tiny smile crossed her face, as she reminisced the occasion. She nodded, but was too overcome to speak.

"Do you know that I'm still crazy about your dimple? And I love how you blush every time I hug you," he teased.

Adhira blushed.

"Yes, like that," he held her chin and pulled her face higher.

"Umm. So, what were you saying? About our first meeting?"

"That you looked heavenly that day," he sounded nostalgic.

"Stop it!" she giggled.

"You look gorgeous when you blush," he smiled and pulled her closer.

"Ok. So what next?" she asked plopping on the red couch that matched her dress.

"Nothing," he replied.

"We eat out? Or do we order food?" As if on cue, her stomach growled.

"No!" he shook his head.

"What do you mean?" she asked again.

"That we do nothing. Let's just dance," he answered, lost in thought.

"How long?" she sensed something wasn't right.

"Forever," he said, simply. "Did you enjoy the wine?" He added.

She nodded.

"Let's have some more." He poured some wine into their glasses.

She took a small sip.

"So what did the doctor say?" she asked.

He looked out of the window, trying to find the right words. He wished he didn't have to utter those words. But she needed to know, she had every right to know.

"That you are dying," his voice trembled.

"What? What do you..." she stammered.

"He said that you are terminally ill, and you have no more than a month to live," he blurted it out, trying to make it less painful for both of them.

"But… but…" She struggled to breathe.

"Are you joking?" she finally asked, trying to make sense of it all.

"No. I'm not." He looked down, fighting his tears.

They held each other's hands and allowed the tears to flow. After a few minutes, she wiped her tears.

Hoping he had an answer, she asked, "What do we do?"

"Nothing. Let's just drink and dance," he looked at her with a longing she had never felt before.

She looked at their glasses and she realized that they were laced with… She knew that he loved her more than anything, more than his own life. This dance was to be their last dance.

She chugged the wine. Finishing his glass, he got up and offered his hand. She took it gently and rested her face on his chest. For one last time, they danced together.

The song had stopped, so he hummed, “Come away with me.”

She whispered, “I’m safe there in your arms.”

The spotlight faded, as the moon eclipsed.

Two Down Three to Go

"I have killed a man!" sitting on the couch, with her eyes closed, she calmly whispers.

I look at her hands to see if they are trembling. This is the first time I hear a murder confession. I need to tread cautiously. Disha has been visiting me for the last year. She wakes up every morning sweating and doesn't remember her dreams.

It is her third hypnotherapy session. In previous sessions, she hasn't provided any details. But today she has nonchalantly slipped into her past life.

I put my notebook aside, take a deep breath and utter the most useless word in the dictionary, "Hmm."

I have to focus and trust my instincts. Nothing I have ever read can help me today. I must prepare myself for the unexpected. How does one even do that? I take a few deep breaths and plunge in.

"What do you see?" I ask, hoping my controlled breathing techniques will suffice to see me through the procedure.

"I see a man in his twenties lying on the floor. He is bleeding profusely," she replies in a steady voice.

"Check his pulse," I almost say her name, but recall just in time, that it is against the fundamental rules of the past life regression hypnotherapy. She may have had a different name in her previous life.

Under the hypnotic spell, she obeys, "No! He is breathing. But he continues to bleed." She sounds upset.

"Argh! My dress is getting dirty," she adds. I notice a frown on her face. Disha sounds more worried about her dress than the dying man.

"What else do you see?" I try to get the details.

"I'm wearing a white dress, a bridal dress. He is wearing a tux. Oh my God! It is our wedding day," raising her eyebrow, she announces.

"How do you know you have assaulted him?" I ask, managing to keep my voice calm, like I am supposed to.

Before she can answer, I offer, "May be someone else did it, and you are just a witness."

"Nope. I am holding the knife," she retorts. "Besides, now I can clearly hear my thoughts."

"What is it that you are thinking?" I ask.

"I am thinking, two down, three to go," she replies with a smirk. I feel sweat trickle down my forehead. I have been worried about her tone so far, but her spine-chilling smirk shakes me to the core.

With no more questions left to ask, I bring her back to the present. As she returns, she does not remember anything about her past life.

"How did it go?" she asks. "Did I see anything today?"

Her goal is to learn from her previous lives and unite the consciousness of past and present lives. But I have to be wary of the repercussions. What if it unleashes the psychopath in her? What if, instead of being therapeutic, it ruins her life?

She is still waiting for her answer. I don't want to lie, but I need time to process all the information, to prepare myself to deal with the situation.

"Umm…" I shrug, and I show her my notebook.

She leaves with an appointment to visit me the next week. I notice a slight smirk on her face. Waving back at her, I most sincerely hope and pray that she is done with all five murders in her previous life.

The End

"Why?" Sagar asked.

His face clouded with despair, as he examined his bloody hands.

Raima was busy, typing on her laptop.

"Go, wash your hands. Then we shall talk," she said, without looking up.

"Look at my hands," he moaned, unable to look away. "They're still dripping blood," he was shocked at her indifference.

"I told you to wash your hands," she clicked her tongue impatiently. "Now be gone until I am done," she replied, peeping through her glasses and gestured towards her laptop.

"Answer me now!" he demanded.

"I know patience is not your strong suite, but can you give me ten minutes?" she adjusted her spectacles, irritably.

"Of course, it's not. Who knows me better than you?" he asked, rhetorically.

He didn't budge, so she stopped typing, "Wash your hands, if it bothers you so much."

"The blood doesn't bother me… murdering her does," his voice trembled.

He asked with tears in his eyes, "Why did you ask me to kill her? You could have helped me patch things up."

"Sit down!" she ordered, slowly reclining against the back of her chair and taking off her glasses.

Sagar sat down and waited for her to speak. She took a moment to clear her thoughts before asking, "Why did you kill her?"

"Because you asked me to," he began, but she interrupted.

"I didn't ask you. You were in a situation, when you came to me. She cheated on you. I told you that there were two choices – move on or take revenge. I never suggested that you kill her," she said, bluntly.

"You visited others before you came to me, right?" she added.

He nodded in reply.

"What did they tell you?" she asked.

"Nothing," he answered looking at his hands.

"I listened to your story. And you blame me?" she raised her eyebrows.

"You think you are the God. Don't you?" he asked, knowing quite well that she was *his* God.

She smiled, "I don't need to answer that. You will be popular, soon. That's what you want. And that's what you deserve."

Wearing her spectacles, she went back to her story –

He loved her. But his jealousy was stronger than his love. In the spur of the moment, he lost himself, and lost everything that mattered to him. Now, he will have to live without her for the rest of his life, and that's what he deserves.

THE END.

With those final words, he vanished.

www.ingramcontent.com/pod-product-compliance
Lightning Source LLC
LaVergne TN
LVHW041100150826
845673LV00007B/1852